ANYTHING

YOU \ I
CAN \ CAN
DO \ DO

Lawrence Ianni

iUniverse, Inc.
Bloomington

Anything You Can Do, I Can Do

This is a work of fiction. All of the characters, names, incidents, organizations, and dialogue in this novel are either the products of the author's imagination or are used fictitiously.

iUniverse books may be ordered through booksellers or by contacting:

iUniverse
1663 Liberty Drive
Bloomington, IN 47403
www.iuniverse.com
1-800-Authors (1-800-288-4677)

ISBN: 978-1-4620-6512-7 (sc)
ISBN: 978-1-4620-6513-4 (e)

Printed in the United States of America

iUniverse rev. date: 12/14/2011

With affection for and appreciation of Sam,
Nick and Paul, my three mentor-brothers

Chapter

I

By time sports columnist Abe Fuller arrived at the City Bar and Grill, the daily hangout of the reporters and feature writers of The Pauliapolis Sentinel, the two tables favored by the journalists were more fully occupied than normal for mid-morning. As he had suspected, a considerable number of his colleagues had come directly from the thought-provoking special staff meeting to air their apprehensions and speculations.

He spotted an empty chair at the table where outdoor editor Arnie Carlson and two metro reporters sat before coffee cups and the remnants of some Danish pastry. Abe sat down without invitation. "Well, Arnie," Abe began as he grinned broadly, "from the look of it, I'd conclude that our fellow journalists are not overjoyed that the management of the paper hired a market research firm to find out how the readers feel about our efforts *to inform and entertain.*" Abe delivered the last phrase with his hands raised and his fingers wiggling to add a quotation mark gesture to the wording of the paper's masthead motto.

Arnie smiled wanly at the four others who had shared the table before Abe Fuller's arrival and said, "Don't you just love Abe's bravado?

I suspect that it's an attempt to mask the massive insecurity we're all feeling."

"Come on, Arnie," Abe responded reassuringly as he looked about for a waitress, you've got nothing to worry about. A few surveys out in the hinterlands and some focus groups composed of townies anxious to get back to their fishing rods and shotguns, and the market researchers will report that your columns pointing our readers toward the ducks and lake trout are admired as brilliant journalism that they can't live without." Having caught the eye of a familiar waitress some distance away, Abe raised Arnie's empty coffee cup in her direction to signal his own desire for coffee.

"Look who's talking," Arnie responded. "You do two columns a week: one on the local minor league baseball team or the national sports scene and the other on the new major league pro football team just organizing for its first season, and people think you're some sort of insightful sports guru."

"You two are about to have your dream worlds shattered," asserted Adele Friedman with a knowing expression before she raised her coffee cup for a sip. Abe looked pointedly toward the next table at the reporter who covered state politics as well as writing a twice weekly column on politics in general. He did not know the pretty, green-eyed reporter well. She had joined the paper's staff just over two years ago. Her appointment had been reacted to with skepticism among the veteran staff because she was only twenty-five at the time and had had only three years experience on a rural daily since graduating from the school of journalism at the University of Missouri. However, she had proven to be a thorough pursuer of meaningful political news and a clear, concise writer. Abe read her political column regularly and found it clever and insightful, though he had never told her that.

Abe had never been troubled with humility, but he suspected himself of being a bit jealous of his attractive colleague. That was why he had never admitted that he assessed the handsome, slightly younger woman as his equal in professional skill. "What dream worlds would those be, Friedman?" Abe asked with clearly communicated doubt. He only conversed with Adele Friedman rarely and briefly. He never discussed matters of substance, which in Abe's case were limited to sports people, sports places and athletic events.

Adele smiled at arts reporter and critic Jay Steinfurth and said, "His innocence is remarkable, isn't it, Jay?" Turning to Abe with the same look that she herself disliked when a politician's staffer displayed it toward her, she said, "Of course the hard core sports junkies are going to tell the market researchers that you two are God's gift to America's true faith, which is to watch games played by pros or by semi-pro college kids and to imagine one is also an athlete by handling the toys of pseudo sports like jet skiing, snow-mobiling and offroading. What you'd better pray is that your readers among the so-called sportsmen and arm chair athletes are numerous enough to convince the publisher that your columns ought to continue."

"You haven't been around long enough to know the demographics, Friedman," Abe responded. His tone had more of the old hand cautioning the rookie than was justified by only seven years more age and professional experience. "In this part of the country, girls first encounter the word 'lure' as a thing at the end of a fishing line long before they're told it's something you do to the opposite sex. And boys get their first shotgun at the same age that they get their first baseball bat. You may be surprised at the size of the sports readership compared to the size of the political readership."

Adele smirked. "I don't need convincing that the captive audience makes writing a sports column a lead pipe cinch, but no ..."

"Wait, wait, wait," interrupted Fuller. "What do you mean a lead pipe cinch? I'll tell you what a lead pipe cinch is. Writing a political column, that's what. Talk about your captive audiences ..."

"Oh, ridiculous," sighed Adele as she leaned back in her chair in mock astonishment. "Let me tell you something ..."

Before she could proceed, Jay Steinfurth got to his feet and pulled on his coat. "I think this is a dispute that I don't need to sit in on." Arnie Carlson reached for his coat as well and told Jay that he would join him in the short walk across the street and down the block to the Sentinel Building. Abe looked about in hopes of some sign that his coffee was on the way. Turning his attention back to Adele, he asserted, "Face it, Friedman, a political column writes itself. In this great country of ours, people take their politics more seriously than their religion. In fact, the two have become inseparable, haven't they? People can't resist reading everything written about politics either in the paper or said in the electronic edition. What they agree with makes them feel secure and what they despise feeds their fears, to which they are addicted as much as to their hopes because the existence of the devil is a part of their religious beliefs. You can write anything about politics and people eat it up."

Adele's amusement was evident. "I don't suppose you see that the necessity to find and communicate the truth imposes any sort of difficulty on the political journalist that sports writers don't have to deal with? In fact, sports writing has just the opposite goal, doesn't it? Hide the flaws and foibles of the public's cherished boy-men to preserve the public's illusions." Adele failed to suppress raising her eyebrows before adding, "It can't be too hard to write an endless series of puff pieces."

"Sports writing can be very hard-hitting when it's called for," Abe retorted, surprised as his defensiveness.

"You mean like your tough piece last month wondering if the Stags ought to give up platooning their two first basemen next season?" Friedman offered with ill-concealed amusement. "I marvel you weren't reprimanded as a consequence of reader outrage."

"I can understand your contemptuous attitude," Abe responded with insincere humility. "You do searing pieces like the one you did on re-districting the southwest suburbs to determine which party will get the advantage in voter registration."

"That piece took a lot of digging, I'll have you know," Adele said with as much defensiveness as Abe had shown.

"O.K." Abe offered with a conciliatory gesture of his hands. "But you will have to admit that writing about politics offers many more opportunities for stories and columns that write themselves than does sports."

"If you tried it, you'd soon find out otherwise." Adele challenged.

"I could handle it a lot more easily than you could write sports," Abe asserted confidently.

"Really?" Adele said with a broad smile that communicated her skepticism.

"Yeh, really," Abe snorted. "I'm willing to put it to the test. I'll write your column under your name for the two weeks of the market research if you'll write mine and we'll see who gets the better survey numbers and reaction feedback when writing for the other person's byline."

"I wouldn't have a career left after two weeks, while yours, on the other hand, would soar," said Adele.

"I figure that I'm the one taking the risk," said Abe. "However, unlike you, I'm not chicken."

"Make it worth my while," Adele challenged. "Say an all expenses paid week in the Caribbean at the loser's expense and you're on."

"What'll determine the winner?" Abe asked.

"The cumulative higher rating for the four columns on the market researchers' five point scale."

"Not good enough," Abe demurred. "The higher number of positive hits to each of our names on the paper's web site should be used too."

"With the negative hits subtracted," Adele qualified.

"And what if the one who's higher in the market survey loses on the web site score, or vice versa?" Abe asked.

"The wider percentage of victory in the part each person won decides," Adele offered.

Abe nodded. He wrote briefly on a sheet he tore from his pocket note pad. He slid the paper toward Adele and got to his feet. "That's my i.d. code so that you can send to the sports editor what you write for my byline. I'm going to go buy some sun screen, a big bottle, I'm going to need it." Adele, who rolled her eyes derisively, did not look intimidated as she wrote down her own i.d. code and handed it to Abe. Abe gave a lighthearted salute as he left.

Chapter

2

Abe exuded confidence the day after he bet Adele Friedman that he could generate more favorable reader reaction when he wrote as her than she could writing as him. He decided on one final scrutiny of his first effort to appear under Adele's byline before sending it on to the computer of the features editor. It began:

Efforts continue to eliminate the existing federal campaign finance reform law. The latest tactic is to encourage a constitutional challenge to the law. The challenge effort is led by Congressman Arden "Lefty" Derwood, the veteran fiscal conservative in all matters except filling his party's campaign war chest to overflowing. Despite recent decisions that have made the existing law almost meaningless, the former major league pitcher asserts that any limitation of campaign contributions is an infringement of free speech. Citing the court's removal of the limitation on corporate contributions, Lefty argues that individuals who have the means and desire to participate in the electoral process financially should not be limited in any way because their doing so is a form of speech which is constitutionally protected.

One wonders if Derwood has given any thought to the consequences of implementing this novel legal reasoning. In this country where access to the media is arguably the most significant factor in the outcome of elections, he would allow the rich to purchase the outcome they desire in every election. That is a kind of freedom unimagined in an important declaration that even the ex-pitcher surely is acquainted with.

Doubtless the congressman knows that money buys elections. His own political career is a result of the increasingly frequent uniting of two factors: celebrity and money. Lefty Derwood had many years of favorable media exposure during his lengthy baseball career. There is obvious political value to that celebrity. Without that favorable visibility from his outstanding athletic career, he never would have been urged by his party to run. The already well-known novice candidate next benefited from a well-funded, carefully managed campaign to convince voters that there was a lot more to Lefty than a live fast ball and a good curve.

Without denigrating the man's intelligence, one asks how a neophyte candidate who spent ages eighteen to thirty-five devoted to professional athletics came to sound passably thoughtful and literate on the complexities of government. Give a candidate a set of statements he believes in, and, if he has a modicum of presence and a fair memory, he should be able to appeal to people already favorably disposed to him and whatever values those statements express. Of course, the voters should not disregard a candidate simply for lack of formal education. Precise, specialized training has never been a firm requirement in our system. For example, the founding fathers did not insist that one had to be a lawyer to serve on the Supreme Court. However, it would be foolish to assert that all life experiences are adequate backgrounds for important political office. A career in professional athletics, which inevitably curtails one's intellectual life, though not necessarily one's attendance in educational institutions, rarely results in splendid qualifications to hold elected office at the federal level or to interpret the constitution, for that matter.

We live in a time when celebrity is such a big advantage in running for office that adding unlimited funding to that advantage makes it increasingly difficult to keep the electoral playing field level. That is the reason that attempts at controlling the funding of the electoral process, admittedly not greatly successful to present, have been made and need to be made much more effective. Maintaining freedom in America has always required restraining the effort to use great financial advantage to gain disproportional favor. That remains a better course of action than to assert some absurd notion that the rich should be free to spend as much as they want to work their will. I hope that none of us ever have to live in a country that uses Lefty Derwood's notion of free speech.

The next day, Arnie skimmed his article published under Adele Friedman's byline with the title he had suggested with his submission, "A Constitutional Wild Pitch." He remained satisfied with his first effort to draw a more favorable appraisal writing as the political columnist than she would produce writing as him. He turned to the sports section to examine what Friedman had produced as a first attempt to write a sports column. He was prepared to be amused. In fact he hoped that she had not done so badly that it would take him some weeks to repair his image; however, he considered that task an acceptable penalty to make his point and enjoy a week in the Caribbean at his colleague's expense, not to mention the months of enjoyable though confidential jibing he intended to administer after his triumph.

Under his byline, Abe saw the title "The Greatest Quarterback Who Never Played the Game." At least she, or the editor, had hit on an intriguing title, he reflected before he began the column itself. It began:

The office of Pauliapolis's expansion pro football franchise, The North Louisiana Loggers, was visited the other day by a member of the commissioner's staff who was assigned to finalize some details of the team's participation in next spring's player draft. He was none other than Mike Mercutio, who had a ten year career as the backup quarterback for the Boston Rebels during the decade when they won four super bowl titles in a ten year period. Mercutio is not a familiar name to many expect the most intense pro football fans because he only played in nine complete games during his entire ten year career. He has four super bowl championship rings although he never played a single play in any of those four Rebel victories. Of course, he is also the only pro quarterback to win every game that he started, a total of nine. Assiduous followers of professional football know this part of the Mike Mercutio career story if they know of him at all. The starting quarterback for the Rebels in their halcyon days was hall of famer Barry Middlebrook, a man with all the tools to be the great pro quarterback that he was. He could hit receivers deep but could also throw short and to the sidelines when the deep coverage was effective. Not to take anything away from his receivers, two of whom have joined him in the hall, Middlebrook was uncanny at seeing all his options. If there was no chance for a quick completion, he had enough speed to run with the ball. Barry the Bomber had such an illustrious career that few remember that his first two seasons were less than sensational because of a full-blown re-building effort on the part of the Rebels.

Mike Mercutio was drafted in case Middlebrook did not realize the potential that had made him a first round draft choice. Mercutio was not a desperation choice. He had had an impressive completion percentage as a college passer. However, his average yardage per completion led to the conclusion that his arm was not strong enough for him to be a top of the line pro quarterback.

The assessment of Mercutio's lack of arm strength was never put to the test for a half dozen seasons as Barry Middlebrook came into his own and led the team to three titles. The Rebels were on their way to a fourth championship when Middlebrook was injured seriously enough in the fifth game of the season to keep him out of action for the next nine games. In came Mike Mercutio to moot all questions about the strength of his passing arm. He led the Rebels through a nine game winning streak, during which his accurate passing coupled with the Rebel trade mark powerful running game made Middlebrook's absence hardly noticed. However, after Barry the Bomber returned for the last two regular season games and through a victorious playoff run which brought the Rebels their fourth super bowl victory, Mike Mercutio's performance was no longer noticed.

Of course, Mercutio picked up his fourth super bowl ring and watched Middlbrook play for three more years to complete his ten year career, but he never played another play. Thus, while it overstates a bit to say Mike Mercutio never played the game, he played so briefly but so well that he doubtless merits the title of The Greatest Quarterback Who Never Played the Game.

Abe was impressed rather than amused. Adele's work was much better than he had expected. He was curious about how she had hit on the subject. Mercutio's playing days had ended over ten years ago. Not only was the commissioner's office half a continent away in Los Angeles, but Mercutio's appointment to it was relatively recent. Friedman had been either incredibly lucky or diligent. Abe would rather that it had been lucky, so he decided to explore his curiosity though it meant admitting to being favorably impressed. Abe checked the internal phone directory taped to the wall beside his desk and punched in Adele Friedman's extension. After two rings Adele responded by stating her name. "Hey, Friedman," Abe began with a tone of voice that labored to be casual, "not a bad column."

"Do you have indigestion, Fuller, or do I detect reluctance to admit that you're impressed?" Adele chuckled. "Tell you what. I'm not a person who takes unfair advantage, I'll call off the bet if you're ready to concede that I can write a sports column better than you can write politics."

"Don't lose your head, Friedman. It's a little early to check the paper's web page to see which of us got more hits on our columns. We'll see whose work was more applauded or trashed. And we won't get the market research results for several days. You may want to run up the white flag then."

"I don't own a white flag; never needed one. Nor expect to now, though I'll admit that your column wasn't as bad as I expected. You were wise to tie into something you're familiar with."

"Familiar territory didn't seem exactly the case with your column," Abe said, his tone now reflecting curiosity rather than the banter of his previous retorts. "How did you hook up with Mike Mercutio for an interview?"

"I just made some calls to find out if anyone interesting was in town. It's called journalism, Fuller. You may have heard of it. Incidentally, I told him that I was doing background for you. You better back me on its being your column even though you hadn't seen him yourself."

"Don't worry; and you do the same if anyone asks you about the baseball tie in if you're asked about what I wrote for you." Abe was still puzzled as to the specificity of what Adele had written. "It must have been a really long interview for you to learn who he was and all about his unusual career."

"Oh, God, Fuller," Adele huffed, "I knew who Mike Mercutio is. If I hadn't, I probably wouldn't have asked for the interview. To anyone who doesn't know his playing career, they'd probably infer that he is some staff functionary with a law degree."

"I didn't know he had a law degree," Abe admitted.

"Well, listen, after our bet is over, I can give you lessons in journalism," Adele offered with elaborate condescension.

"You're pretty cocky for someone who hasn't even checked the web site yet, let alone gotten the market research feedback."

"I think I'll look at the web site right now, unless there's something else you wanted to say, like a brief statement of surrender?"

Abe made a scoffing noise. "I've just one more thing to say. I'll be here for a while in case you want to call back with a concession statement after you check the web site."

Adele was still chuckling when she cut Abe off.

Chapter

3

be was as curious as Adele to see the number and content of the hits that the two columns had drawn to the Sentinel's web page. What he found did not make him happy. He was not surprised that the column that he had written for Adele's byline had drawn a number of negative reactions from political conservatives who viewed any criticism of a conservative lawmaker as requiring a vituperative response. Even if the opinion expressed was one that might hold some cogency for citizens of a variety of political views, conservative citizens were bound to respond against any criticism of a right wing officeholder.

To them, any criticism was another example of a liberal bias in the press that could not be let stand unresponded to. Thus, while campaign finance reform was a change desired by the vast majority of the electorate, criticism of Congressman Lefty Derwood for standing on the first amendment, even if on dubious grounds, had to be attacked. Abe could have written himself most of those castigations of Adele Friedman for his piece as her for the column's supposed bias against conservative views. However, the political views of the region, ignoring registration figures, were by majority moderate to liberal. Hence, Abe anticipated that a column devoted to condemning an attempt to torpedo campaign finance reform on dubious constitutional grounds would draw more favorable reactions than it did predictable negative ones. In fact, the negative comments outnumbered the favorable ones by three to one, 118 to 39.

The reactions to Adele's column under his byline increased his displeasure, although their overwhelmingly favorable nature would have delighted him if he had actually written the piece himself. Not only were the total of 47 reactions a larger number reacting to the column than would be normal for one of his pieces, they were unanimously favorable. Even the profile of those readers who had taken the trouble to write was interesting. Many of them described themselves as truly committed football fans who prided themselves in knowing who Mike Mercutio was. These respondents asserted that casual fans could never identify the man who had four super bowl rings though he had not appeared in a super bowl game. Only true devotees remembered the season where Mercutio had come off the bench and performed so admirably that his hall of fame predecessor was hardly missed.

An even more frequent theme was to applaud the human dimension of the column. These comments endorsing a column that discussed a workman athlete who had used his moment well and gone on to make a successful professional career after his playing days. Where Abe would have otherwise glowed with pride, he choked with frustration at the plaudits Adele's column written for his signature had garnered. He pinned his hopes for some relief from his annoyance on the outcome of the market research, which would be based on scientifically designed demographic samples rather that the compilation of voluntarily initiated reactions.

Two days later, he found a little, but less than sufficient comfort from the market research results. His piece had done especially well with those who described themselves as registered voters who voted regularly. Abe was comforted that the unsolicited negative reaction to his piece about a political conservative's attempt to scuttle campaign finance reform came entirely from a group of voters whose political orientation did not fit into the mainstream of either party as a portion of a scientific sample of the region's registered voters,

Two thirds of the market researchers' sample agreed with the views expressed in the column Abe had written under Adele Friedman's byline. Furthermore, a substantial majority did not find the harsh negative characterization of ex-jocks in politics inappropriate. Although few of them were aware of the former major league pitcher who was now a conservative congressman in another state, he was not appraised favorably on first acquaintance with him through the column. The correlation between wealth and conservative political views was a perception that was endorsed by the respondents without any allowance for rich ex-athletes who had entered politics. The overall rating of the column was 4.1 on the 5 point scale.

All of the data encouraged Abe's optimism about the outcome of the first encounter in his contest with Adele until he looked at the comments and numerical evaluation regarding her piece written under his byline. Not only were the comments nearly unanimously favorable, a small portion of the sample stated that they normally did not read sports columns but had read and enjoyed this one after its title had caught their eye. The overall numerical rating for the piece was 4.0.

Abe read the favorable comments with a mixture of envy and chagrin. When he had read all he could stand, he glanced toward the other side of the meeting room in which the market researchers were presenting their results to the assembled journalists. Adele was looking his way with a broad smile on her face. She must have kept her eyes toward him for his inevitable glance in her direction. As Abe looked at her dourly, Adele raised her near arm vertical from the elbow to the hand. She wriggled her fingers in a motion of greeting. From the gesture together with her smile, Abe got the message of triumphant amusement. Abe acknowledged her wave with a curt nod of his head and turned away. Before he did his next column under the woman's byline, he decided, a little research of his own was called for.

Not much research was necessary to stir Abe's competitive mettle. The biographical sketch of Adele Friedman on paper's web site, which Abe had never looked at before, sent him to the web site of the rural daily in South Dakota which had first employed her out of journalism school. She had joined that paper still carrying her maiden name, which was Castle. To the veteran sports writer, the name rang a bell for two reasons. There was a legendary high school football coach named Castle who was still coaching in one of the small towns of South Dakota, Prairie View.

Furthermore, Abe recalled, Coach Castle had a daughter, Addie Castle, who owned the career high scoring record for college basketball players in South Dakota, not just for women college basketball players, but for all college basketball players. Checking again on Friedman's listed place of birth, there either had been two Adele Castles of similar age in the metropolis of Prairie View or Adele Friedman was the reigning scorer in the history of South Dakota college basketball.

Fuller reflected with astonishment. He was being conned by an ex-jock who was not only familiar with team sports since childhood but knew an athlete's mentality from her own stellar accomplishments. He punched in Adele Friedman's extension number with considerably more force than necessary.

When Adele answered simply with her last name, Fuller said, "Oh, I'm sorry; I was calling Addie Castle. Is she in?" he asked with as much sarcasm as he could muster.

"I hope you're not expecting an award for investigative journalism for having learned that information," Adele answered with amusement that conveyed no element of distress.

"No, no," Abe countered, "I just wanted you to know that I know the kind of devious person I'm dealing with."

"Oh. please, was I supposed to tell you that I know that most game balls are blown up instead of stuffed?"

Abe labored at trying to sound injured. "I just think that an honest person would have disclosed a couple of things as relevant to our little contest, such as daddy's nodding acquaintance with football and your having played a little basketball."

"Has it been your experience that being a jock gives one an edge in being a sports writer?" Adele scoffed.

"I don't have to explain the phrase 'a level playing field' to you, do I?" his tone of injured gravity failing at sincerity. "I guess there was no course in ethics in the j-school curriculum at Missouri."

"Don't get carried away, Fuller," Adele snorted. "Or should I ask if you have any cuttings of that political column called *The Fuller Report* that you used to write when you were a rookie in Kansas?"

"Why should I have mentioned that? I just filled in for a couple of months while the regular guy was recuperating from a heart attack."

"Perhaps you're right," Adele offered with faux agreeability. "If I got to read some of your stuff, I'd probably agree that the experience gave you no advantage in our little contest. Might have increased my feeling of the certainty of victory, in fact."

"You know, Friedman, you can be a pain in the ass without exerting a whole lot of effort."

"Ah, crudeness," Adele said brightly, "the eventual resort of someone of limited wit." With that she cut off.

Abe stared at the phone in his hand and decided he had not taken the contest with Adele Friedman seriously enough. The possibility of paying for her to vacation for a week was now the least of the reasons he wanted to win the contest. The woman was badly in need of some humility.

Chapter

4

After a half hour of fruitless cogitation on a winning topic for his second political column under the Friedman byline, Abe decided to look at the latest wire service transmissions. He was no longer trying to find a subject that would be responded to more favorably than what Adele would write under his name. He just wanted something that would not be embarrassing to either Adele or himself. The latter, he had to admit, was very important to him. He had to admit that he wanted the woman's respect. It was, he had to concede, more important to him than besting her in their contest. He grunted disappointingly. None of the major wire stories seemed to include a topic that struck him as having potential for a column of commentary.

As he almost finished a quick skimming of the lengthy list of brief items, none of them more than a couple of sentences, his eye was caught by a three line item that came out of California. It said that a group was considering another try at a ballot initiative to create exceptions to the state's term limits law. Abe recalled that there had been an earlier ballot initiative to establish the exception that had failed. Its intent was to permit a legislator who was serving his or her last eligible term to run for the same seat again if the percent of the total vote he or her has attained in his or her last election had been 75% or more of the votes cast. The reasoning behind the proposed change was that any incumbent who could attain such a plurality, in this case three-fourths or more of the votes cast, had some bipartisan acceptability. Therefore, the voters of that district should be permitted to decide by majority vote if they wanted that legislator to serve again. Recalling that this modification of California's term limits law had been unsuccessfully proposed a few years ago, Abe recognized a topic worthy of comment. He began a draft which eventually appeared with the title "Line Iteming Term Limits."

Once again a signature drive is under way in California to put a ballot initiative before the voters to make exceptions to the state's term limits legislation. The proponents of this legislation remind me of my sorority sisters in college. The organization had a rather clearly stated set of rules specifying a member's financial and behavioral obligations to the group. No one had ever been sanctioned for violating them, however. The group always changed the rules if someone were actually in violation of some obligation. The exception was always made because the offender was likeable or extraordinary skillful in arranging activity that involved either male students or alcohol or both. Thus, some voters in California, now confronted with losing the services of some incumbents of whom they highly approve, would like to create legal exceptions to permit these office holders to continue to be eligible to be re-elected.

The argument is that a district should not lose the services of an able legislator simply because his or her time has expired under the term limits law. Of course the argument is not new. When term limits were first proposed, one of the most cogent arguments against the policy was that effective, highly experienced public servants should not be lost to the public just when their experience had made them most useful to the public interest. Obviously there were counter arguments that carried the day at that time. The liabilities of an office holder's long time entrenchment, such as obligations to donors, deafness to the concerns of constituents (even those of his own party), and especially the abuse of the powers that accumulate with incumbency were felt by a majority of California voters to outweigh the positive values of prior good service. So term limits were enacted in California.

The feared negative consequences of term limits have inevitably arrived. Particular legislative districts have lost representatives who were deemed to understand and deliver on the district's needs and desires in particularly effective fashion. Their successors have not sometimes been as effective in providing either pork or principles; hence the new idea of term limits with exceptions has arisen. Of course, voters have always had a means of limiting terms without there being legal limits. It is called an election. However, because the electorate is usually unwilling to exercise voluntary restraint, they have tried to force restraint upon themselves by legal means.

It is a rare law that will not cut both ways to some extent. When the undesirable consequences of the law manifests themselves, that is when the citizens of a democracy need to muster their maturity and conclude that the positive results of the law so outweigh the liabilities that they will continue to support the law and not emasculate it into insignificance. Unfortunately, the citizenry sometimes displays immaturity rather than grown up judgment and sacrifices constructive change to foolish willfulness.

A perfect example of this sacrifice of the greater good to the preservation of willfulness is the fate of the briefly existing law which created the line item veto. It only requires a recollection of the recent past to remember the line item veto. It established that the president of the United States could veto specific items within a spending bill rather than exercising the traditional prerogative to either sign or veto a bill in its entirely. The congressional majority which conceived the line item veto and passed it no doubt envisioned that a president of their party would be able to excise the opposition's pork or pet items and expeditiously set the government to functioning. It would not be necessary, in other words, to return an entire budget bill to the congress for the long and often wasteful process of working out a mutually agreeable set of pork and pet items so that the congress could forward a bill that the president could sign in toto. The legislation also provided that the congress could override the president's line item vetoes with a majority somewhat larger than the usual simple majority. On the whole, the line item legislation was a means to make government more efficient and less wasteful.

The lifetime of the line item veto was very short. The party which conceived the legislation found that a president of the opposition party was using the line item veto to excise some expenditures dear to their hearts and necessary more for building good will with donors and special interest groups (not that any one party has a monopoly on such items.) With this striking development manifest to their horror, the very people who conceived the line item veto killed it.

When the demise of the line item veto occurred, no doubt many people were puzzled and wondered why the bill's proponents did not anticipate that the law would occasionally work to their displeasure? Those who ask that question forget to account for the presence of that portion of humanity who see nothing but the up side of any course of action. Amazingly, a large number of these sunny-side-only people run for public office. It is almost a requirement. That way, they can believe that term limits will only effect someone else's length of public service.

After Abe sent the column on for editorial scrutiny, he savored a moment of unalloyed satisfaction. He sometimes not fully satisfied with a piece of writing although he sent it on for publication. He often passed on his work in agreement with the French writer who said that one does not finish one's work, one abandons it. The sentiment was emphatically true for newspaper columnists who live with deadlines constantly hovering more closely than for any other writer. Yet only occasionally did one feel totally satisfied with a piece, convinced that it was exactly what one wanted to say. Of such pieces, it did not matter whether any other person liked it, the writer was satisfied with it. The opinions and analysis might not be unassailable, but they were totally reflective of the writer's intent.

Of course, since it would carry Adele Friedman's name, he hoped she did not dislike it intensely, but even then he would make no apologies for it. As to the reader reaction that would be reported by the market researchers, he did not care whether or not it outpolled Adele's effort that would carry his name. The content mirrored his convictions. What more could any writer want?

Chapter

5

Abe got a last minute assignment to cover what he considered a non-event, the monthly meeting of the North Louisiana State University board of trustees, so he had not read Adele's effort that carried his name when he arrived at the board meeting in the morning. After several people told him that they liked his column, his curiosity drove him to get a discarded copy of the Sentinel and read what Adele had written for him. He smiled as he saw the heading. The topic was one that sports writers across the country regularly dealt on at intervals whenever one of baseball's most revered records was being threatened with revision. The title was: The Greatest Baseball Player of All Times?

As was to be expected, after Jose Valenzuela of the recently returned for the dead Pittsburgh Pirates hit the 650th home run of his career the other night, speculation has begun that the young outfielder would one day break Barry Bonds' home run record. The more rash among the commentators, projecting the number of years his career is likely to continue, have begun to call him the greatest player who ever played the game.

We are not very far removed from the time when Barry Bonds was called the greatest player of all times when he set the current career home

21

run record. I have always been fond on the stand that Scott Ostler of the San Francisco Chronicle took at the time when Bonds was crowned "the Greatest" by some other sports writers. Ostler stated that, home run output notwithstanding, no one else can be compared to Babe Ruth as the greatest baseball player of all time. He reasoning was simple and incontestable as supported by the facts. If one defines a baseball player as someone who excels at a range of skills used in the game rather than solely hitting, Ruth is in a class by himself. Try to think of another player who pitched twenty victories in a season and also in other years lead the league in home runs. (In Ruth's case a high of sixty in one season.) There are, of course, no others. Hence, by Ostler's definition of greatness, one cannot deny his assertion that Ruth is the greatest baseball player of all times.

There is a caveat one may explore about Scott Ostler's conclusion. It is that, at the time of Ruth's accomplishments, the color line in baseball had not yet been broken. If it had, Ruth would have had a couple competitors as the greatest. For those who determine "the greatest" simply on home runs, neither Ruth nor Bonds, with their sixty and seventy-three respectively, would have had the single season home run record. The great Negro League long ball hitter Josh Gibson would still own that one with a total of seventy-five. As to the all-around player recognition, the competitor is Ted Radcliffe, whom Damon Runyon nicknamed Double Duty Radcliffe the year he batted .325 as a catcher and had a pitching record of 19-8. Radcliffe's career of more than two decades was with the Pittsburgh Crawfords, a team he served as pitcher, catcher and manager. It is not reported whether or not he collected tickets before the games, but I doubt it since, as a catcher, he was probably warming up the starting pitcher. Radcliffe's career overlapped with the latter part of Ruth's, after Ruth left the mound for the outfield. But for that and the color line, which was broken when Radcliffe was forty-four, the pair could have gone head-to-head to resolve the question of who was the greatest baseball player of all time.

Abe smiled as he put down the sports page. He wished he had written Adele's piece, which was the ultimate complement that one writer can pay to another. He was even fonder of Adele's piece that went to his credit when he looked at the web site reactions and the market research data. While his column written for Adele's byline was complimented favorably by a margin of 81 to 19 random reactors,

Adele's for him drew 57 favorable reactions without a single negative comment. On the other hand, in the market researchers' carefully selected demographic sampling, what was described as the thought-provoking nature of what he had written was accorded a 4.6 rating, while Adele's sentimental piece was rated a 4.0. Reflecting on the frigidity of the usual North Louisiana winter, Abe thought he could feel a bit of the warm Caribbean sun on his shoulders.

On his third attempt to call Adele, she picked up and responded with her last name. With equal terseness, he said, "It's Fuller."

"Aw, why am I not surprised at your call," she said. "You wanted to be sure that the market research scores have been called to my attention."

"Not my purpose," Abe responded mildly. "I wanted to tell you how much I liked your piece."

"You're not on your game, Fuller. I almost can't detect the sarcasm," Adele said without a trace of annoyance.

"That's because none was intended," Abe said. "Don't be so suspicious. Your point was well taken and nicely expressed."

There was a brief pause and Adele said, "Thanks. Yours was the same. I am still a fan of the line item veto."

"Well, thank you, Friedman. That's decent of you."

"You're welcome, Fuller. But don't get any illusions. Next week's two columns are going to send you down," Adele said with certainty.

"That'll never happen. You better start scaring up my vacation money, Friedman. I don't do Spartan accommodations." Abe hung up, not wanting to risk another exchange.

Chapter

6

Abe chose boldness for his next piece under Adele's byline. He aimed for a strong favorable response from independent political thinkers. His effort entitled "Do Political Parties Exist?" appeared in the next day's Sentinel.

The ink was barely dry on the campaign finance reform law and the major political parties found ways to circumvent it. Astonishingly, the flood of money that is being spent in election campaigns has continued to increase. Hence, we can be sure that the disproportional influence on government by major contributors will also increase. By merely lodging contributions in the hands of state party organizations rather than the national party, the major parties are able to amass the enormous amounts of money that the reform legislation was intended to prevent. This tactic, as well as the use of the so-called issue organizations that in theory do not endorse candidates, continues to swell campaign expenditures.

The people who believed it foolish or unlawful to attempt to control the financial aspect of elections are already reciting their "I told you so's." But before we give up on rescuing the political process from the corrupting power of money, it may be wise to consider a more fundamental tactic for attacking the problem that has not yet been tried. The intent of campaign finance reform is basically an attempt to control the behavior of political parties. Recognizing this intent inevitably raises a question: how does one control the behavior of political entities that are not recognized to exist in the basic law of the land? The constitution of the United States does not recognize the existence of political parties even though they are the fundamental mechanism in the process that determines the political leadership and laws by which we live. Most Americans, if they bother to vote at all, give little thought to their political philosophy except the name of the party to which they explicitly or tacitly belong. They perceive who will be a good or bad elected official on the basis of that person's party membership irrespective of what the person actually has done to qualify him or her for public responsibility. In addition, the electorate's assumption about what the candidate will do in office is based on party affiliation.

The electorate's approval or disapproval of the behavior of an incumbent office holder is rationalized on the basis of the elected official's party membership. If one shares party membership with a candidate, his relentless fund raising is seen simply the reality that must be engaged in to get elected. If he or she is of the opposition, the candidate is judged as having sold out to special interests. For really extreme party loyalists, elected officials of the opposition party become demons, incapable of judicious action. "My candidate wants to do the right thing; your candidate simply responds to the polls," says the party loyalist when opposing candidates share the same position on an issue.

Yet, despite political parties being the telescope through which most people see all things political, mention of these organizations is nowhere to be found in our constitution as established entities with a defined role in the American electoral process. Political parties were not envisioned as necessary or facilitative mechanisms when the constitution was written. When parties soon arose out of shared positions on a specific issue, some of the most influential of the founding fathers thought political parties were a bad idea. Indeed, their experiences in the early days of the republic did much to confirm their fears about the divisiveness and underhandedness that concerted political action would lead to.

For better or worse, political parties became entrenched mechanisms and are apparently here to stay. (Frankly, it is hard to imagine how such a vast political entity such as America would work without such organizations.) They may change their names and their positions; in fact, they may completely reverse themselves on an issue from one generation to another, seeing as wisdom what was once anathema to the party loyalists.

Since the necessity of political parties is manifest, isn't it time that their existence and their role in the electoral process should be written into the constitution? If we are to have any chance at all of controlling their excesses, from their being overly solicitous to their contributors, to using unscrupulous campaign tactics, to their having made it impossible for a person of modest means to run for office, must we not first recognize that they exist and define in law what their function will be?

No doubt there are those who would argue that it is unnecessary that the country have a constitutional amendment to recognize the right of the people to organize political parties. After all, some aspects of the role of these entities in the electoral process is recognized in many pieces of legislation that explicitly or implicitly recognize their existence. Besides, there are centuries of tradition that establish their functioning as part of the country's political processes.

The established tradition argument does nothing to satisfy anyone who has thought about the ways that the traditions have distorted our democracy in ways that a thoughtful person would wish otherwise. Consider, for example, the way in which electors, the people who technically elect the president, are themselves selected. The framers did not envision these individuals as committed to one party or another. Hence it was not considered that the choice of them was an all or none party outcome. If the framers had recognized the emergence of a multiple number of political entities, they might have arranged to apportion electors rather than our having the all or none arrangement we have fallen into. A majority of the popular vote in a state grants a political party the confirmation of its entire slate of electors. Yet if electors were granted proportionally in reflection of the popular vote, the national outcome could be quite different in instances where large pluralities in one state offset close losses in another state.

Notice that third parties are never granted a portion of electors unless that party carries a state, even if millions of people may have voted for that party's candidate. If that party did receive some electors in reflection of the popular vote, that party would have a voice in the choice of the president that it is now denied. Currently, that denial makes supporting a third party candidate a waste of a vote in most instances. Wouldn't the legitimacy of our democracy be improved by such a change?

No doubt many would assert that the existing arrangement has served well for over two centuries. (The truth of that assertion requires overlooking two instances when the elector tally was at variance with the popular vote.) They would argue that the traditional mechanism is both dynamic and flexible, and a constitutional amendment recognizing the role of political parties might lead to rigidity and stagnation. The only way to put that assertion to the test is to put a well-formulated amendment on the role of political parties before the states and see if thirty-eight of them will ratify it.

When the newly printed Sentinel came to Abe's hand, he opened it to the editorial page to confirm that his piece written for Adele's byline was actually there. This was a ritual Abe religiously performed regarding whatever news story or column he had written. It was as though he had to look through the hospital nursery window to confirm that his child had been born. After a mere glance at his work he hurried on to the sports section to examine Adele's piece under his byline. It was a peculiar feeling to hope that what was in print attributed to him would seem less attractive to him and the paper's readers than his own writing that would be attributed to Adele. Abe considered if one's secret pride in what one had actually written could be satisfying even if one also had to hope that the writing was publicly attributed to oneself was less attractive to readers than his own work that was attributed to someone else.

Abe suppressed his mental ambivalence before dwelling on the paradox would have him wallowing in regret that the contest with Adele had ever been undertaken. However, before he could begin to read Adele's piece entitled "Sports Straws in the Political Wind," his phone rang and he responded with his last name as a greeting. The managing editor informed him that he wanted to talk to him immediately about his column. Abe reacted like a hungry man whose favorite sandwich had just slipped from his grasp and hit the floor. Though the editor's voice conveyed neither anger nor enthusiasm, Abe was immediately apprehensive. Henry Burton was well known for inscrutability whether his summons were prompted by crisis or routine; however, caution was always called for by his requests to meet.

Abe requested a few minutes delay before appearing at the editor's office, so that he could read the column that Adele had written, which he now expected to submerge him in some very hot water. He pondered the intriguing title for a moment and then began to read.

Our North Louisiana senior U.S. senator, Randall E. Brockhurst, cast the deciding vote the other day on a decision in the senate Public Works Committee meeting which will have significant consequences, not only for him, for our city of Pauliapolis, and for the residents of other cities around the country that have or want to acquire professional sports teams. The consequences will be immediate for Brockhurst and Pauliapolis, although they will be more gradual in impacting the other cities in question. Senator Brockhurst cast the deciding vote in an otherwise evenly split committee against releasing a bill proposed by California Senator Carlos Rodriguez that would prohibit the use of public funds to finance the construction of any facility for use by a professional athletic team.

There has been considerable interest in Pauliapolis for building a new football stadium to be the home of our recently organized pro football team, the North Louisiana Loggers. An intense competition was waged among a half dozen cities to be awarded the first expansion of "major league" pro football available in many years. The agreement that the Loggers owners had already secured with North Louisiana State University to use its football stadium for professional games was an essential element in making their bid for the franchise successful because none of the other competitors had an existing adequate stadium in hand.

However, once the franchise was awarded, local sentiment developed for a new, state of the art stadium to serve as a more proper home for the new team. Talk of a combination of private and public funding to underwrite the construction of a domed stadium to serve as a home for the Loggers was almost immediate. Local enthusiasm for football being what it is, there is considerable support and little opposition to the stadium or funding its construction partially or wholly with public money. It seems therefore quite likely that a measure will appear on the next local election ballot asking public approval of an earmarked and set term tax increase to fund the city's portion of a stadium project.

In these days when most cities cannot manage to provide a good and relatively cheap public transportations system, putting a city's always limited revenues into a stadium or arena can be considered a misplacement of priorities. To increase the tax burden of the entire constituency when not everyone is a sports fan, incredible as that may seem to committed fans, might be argued as poor public policy in these money-conscious times.

It is in response to these complex concerns that Senator Rodriguez drafted his bill. Let those who will reap the profits bear the cost of housing their enterprise, asserts the senator. Those of us who enjoy or, like your writer, earn their living in one of the numerous peripheral activities to professional sports may be concerned that professional sports cannot thrive without public financial support. However, continuing the tradition of tax support for professional sports facilities merits thorough examination. The subject will not receive that extensive consideration at this time, however. Rodriguez's bill had to be voted out of the Public Works committee to make it to the floor of the senate and receive the full consideration that it merits.

It will not emerge from the committee because our own Senator Brockhurst cast the deciding vote against releasing the bill in an otherwise evenly split committee. Certainly Brockhurst's action will be popular here in the state of Northern Louisiana and particularly so here in Pauliapolis. His vote may well have been against the long term public interest, despite its popularity in this state and with the owners of sports franchises.

In searching for reasons why Senator Brockhurst chose to prevent a broad consideration of taxing the public to support profit making sports, one is led to two possibilities. The obvious one is that the senator wants to please the voters in Pauliapolis and to a lesser extent those of the whole state. The other possibility is more speculative yet more intriguing. Rumor has it that Brockhurst may try for his party's presidential nomination in the campaign three years hence. If that is the case, his popularity within the state and with his own party could bring him a favorite son endorsement from his party's North Louisiana delegation at its national convention. In addition, the deep pockets of the professional sports owners and their equally affluent friends could go a long way to launching a candidate from a state with a relatively small population and few major donors into the expensive realm of presidential politics.

Abe felt ambivalent when he finished the piece. He was not embarrassed but a little worried to have the piece appear under his byline. Then he admitted that that sentiment was dishonest. The piece was laden with positions and inferences that he wished he could truly take credit for. Adele had a real journalist's nose for news. He doubted he would have noticed Brockhurst's committee vote that was so significant for the local pro sports scene. He had himself several times in the past two years written on the financial complexities of funding pro sports stadiums. It was an issue that would require searching nationwide consideration in the near future. Not only was it a piece that Abe was comfortable to meet with the editor about, but he could imagine no reason for Senator Brockhurst to be discomforted by the article.

Just to be on the safe side, however, Abe decided to seek Adele's view on the reason for the editor's wanting to discuss the column. He called and got her voice mail. Abe did not think he could delay his going to the editor's office until he could track Adele down and ask her if there anything problematical that had emerged in her research for the column or whether she may have heard any adverse reaction to the piece that would prompt a summons to the editor's office. He could infer no legitimate reason that the column had been troublesome to anyone. As a delaying tactic, he decided that he would just stand on his journalist's prerogative to respect the confidentiality of sources if there was some farfetched reason for a complaint.

Henry Burton showed his usual outward placidity as he invited Abe to sit down in the chair opposite his desk. "Good column in today's paper, Abe," Burton said.

"I thought it worked out pretty well," Abe responded. He did not want to express too much pride over something he had not actually written. However, Burton was known for the infrequency of his praise, despite his evident respect for his reporters and columnists, so Abe felt obliged to be somewhat responsive.

"Something unusual has developed from appearance of your column," Burton said and paused. He looked at Abe and seemed to expect a query. Abe knew that an expression of curiosity would start the dialogue toward the editor's control. Both the reporter and the former reporter knew that sometimes silent eye contact was the wisest question one could ask.

After a full length poker table pause, Burton decided he did not want to play. "Senator Brockhurst's office called," the editor reported.

"Surely not to assert there's a factual error?" Abe responded. He had enough faith in Adele Friedman's meticulousness to give his question a confident air.

Burton gave a reassuring negative shake of his head. "No factual inaccuracy was claimed."

Abe was affronted on Adele's behalf and asked pointedly, "How could they possibly complain about a reasonable discussion of a vote on the public record about a prominent issue? The only extrapolations in the piece are the implications for Brockhurst's chances if he runs for the presidential nomination, which has been rumored for months, and never been denied by the senator or his staff at that."

"Brockhurst's office hasn't complained about anything," Burton offered with the faintest of smiles. Abe's puzzled expression prompted Burton to continue. "They have made a request and I thought it best to discuss it with you before the paper acceded to it."

"I can't imagine what they want."

"They'd like a complete account of whatever reaction the paper gets to your column," Burton said without the least indication of how he felt about the request.

"You mean the hits on my web address?" Abe asked. To Burton's affirmative nod, Abe continued, "I doubt that I could claim them as personal property, but surely the paper can."

"They are really accessible to anyone who's moderately enterprising, although the paper could assert a claim to ownership," Burton said. "However, J. A. isn't interested in denying the senator the information."

Abe smiled knowingly. The mention of the paper's owner, J. Ambrose Etheridge, led Abe to an obvious inference. "I take it that this request didn't come directly to you."

Burton looked at Abe with a bland expression and said, "Let's for the sake of simplicity say that it did." The fundamental fiction regarding the Pauliapolis Sentinel was that owner and publisher Ambrose Etheridge never intruded into the operation of the paper. Abe accepted that part of Burton's job description was to maintain that fiction. He was too much of a realist to think less of the editor for it. With a sardonic grin, Abe said, "Let me take a wild guess. The senator's staff is aware of our on going market research. That data, of course, is much more useful as information on how the senator's vote on the stadium bill is playing than just random hits on a web site."

Burton retained his bland expression. "You obviously recognize that the paper could give out that data without our having this discussion."

"Why are we having this discussion?" Abe asked with genuine curiosity.

"It would be desirable if you were not to make an issue of the release of the data to the senator's office," Burton said with his usual flare for understatement.

"Come on, chief," Abe smiled mirthlessly, "any complaint I would made wouldn't have any impact. As you pointed out, it's the paper's data."

"Still," Burton admitted, "it is a little early for the paper to be seen as cooperating so freely with anyone's presidential aspirations, no matter how tentative they may be." That's why the publisher doesn't want there to be any public notice of our providing data to Brockhurst. You know how leaks seem to occur when someone is distressed."

Abe mugged wide-eyed innocence. "I have heard of such shocking events. However, there's no danger in this instance." Abe spoke reassuringly, but shifted quickly to an earnest mode. "But it does seem to me that a little quid pro quo is in order."

"Like what?" Burton asked suspiciously.

"We ought at least to get an interview with Brockhurst about whether he'll try for the nomination."

"It's too early for a dark horse like him to commit," Burton said, adding with a touch of pedantry, "you ought to know that."

Abe responded boldly, a scheme that might be to his advantage suddenly occurring to him. "If he has the caginess that he'll need to go for the nomination as a long shot contender, he ought to be able to say as much as would help him while avoiding too early an exposure."

Burton clenched his mouth and raised his chin indicating thoughtful agreement, evidently impressed with his reporter's perception. "Maybe he should get you to manage his campaign. Still," Burton added, "I'm not sure it's a good idea for you to do a political interview."

"I'm not without experience, you know. I covered politics before you hired me."

"I know," Burton said. "That's why we hired you to do sports. You haven't forgotten the political uproar you caused there, I trust?"

"Ancient history. This interview would be a follow up to my column," Abe argued, surprising himself in the ease that he adopted Adele's work as his own.

Burton chose to be blunt, "You seem to be the one who's unable to put ancient history behind you. One would think that you were the only journalist in history that got fired over bold political coverage, appropriate though his coverage may have been."

"Maybe I need to get back on the horse, as the saying goes, to put the past behind me," Abe reasoned. "Why waste a good follow up opportunity that I generated for myself." Abe labored not to betray the guilt that he felt at his deception. However, he felt sincere about this being a chance to bury a painful aspect of his past.

Burton studied the reporter silently for a time. "You're right. It would be foolish to waste an opportunity. I'll give Friedman the assignment if Brockhurst grants the interview," Burton said decisively.

Abe was tempted to argue further, but he did not want to overplay his hand. If his manipulation to get the assignment to write on a hot topic for his last column under Adele's signature had succeeded, then he would have felt some guilt that Adele would lose the opportunity that she herself had really created. A committed political reporter working in a small state market did not get many chances to do first hand writing about presidential politics. Maybe Adele should not lose the opportunity because of their wager. Maybe he should propose calling off the next round of their writing for each other's bylines to give Adele her chance.

He decided it would be wise to warn Adele that Burton might succeed in arranging the interview with Senator Brockhurst before the editor's call giving Adele the assignment would take her by surprise. With a brief statement that he phrased to sound like disappointed resignation, Abe exited Burton's office quickly.

When he briefly informed Adele that he had proposed the interview but that she would be assigned it if Brockhurst acceded, she responded with a single word, "Idiot."

"Whoa," Abe objected, "try to restrain your appreciation. I thought you'd love the chance."

"Why should I appreciate your setting me up to listen to an hour or more of self-serving pap from someone who wants me to push along his dark horse candidacy for his party's presidential nomination?" Adele asked with emphatic distaste.

"No one says you've got to do a puff piece," Abe countered.

"Come on," Adele shot back. "After the 'off the records' and the 'not for attributions' what will be left to write except hints that the good senator, if sufficiently urged, may bestow on the electorate his availability to run for the presidency?"

"Somewhere, I'd picked up the impression that a good journalist could get to the story that should be told even if it's not the one that the interviewee wants to have told."

"Oow," cooed Adele, adopting a round-eyed expression of feigned astonishment. "Listen to the sports writer explaining journalism to someone who actually does it."

Abe's irritation showed immediately. "Yeh, well this sports writer did his turn at political writing while you were still in j school, and maybe knows things about it that you haven't learned yet."

Adele sensed she had touched a sore point, but before she could say anything conciliatory, Abe had disappeared from her cubical.

Chapter

7

Adele had not been able to muster any enthusiasm when Henry Burton told her that she had been scheduled to interview Senator Randall E. Brockhurst. Nor was her enthusiasm increased when she was informed that she would be taking with her the survey results and web site reactions to the column that appeared under Abe Fuller's signature on the senator's vote which killed the bill to prohibit public funding for professional sports stadiums.

She dutifully entered the federal building in downtown Pauliapolis and made her way through security and the maze of corridors to the senator's suite of offices that occupied a corner of the first floor. The location allowed a spacious staff and visitor waiting area separate from the senator's inner sanctum. The amount of space and the advantageous location spoke to the veteran senator's clout in the pecking order of the state's elected officials. The furnishings of the outer office were not expensive looking but looked substantial. The equipment was extensive and state of the art. The number of staffers was more numerous than Adele expected. North Louisiana was not a populous state. There was probably frequent visitor traffic because the senator's office was in the state's only major population center; however, if the other two visitors of the moment in addition to her were the normal burden, the number of staff was more than ample. Of course, Brockhurst's seniority in the senate accorded him several important committee assignments. Perhaps that necessitated more than usual staffing. On the other hand, perhaps the possibility of a run for the senator's party's presidential nomination was the reason for some of the staffing. After an announcement of candidacy, such staffing would be moved to a campaign office and paid from different funds, if such was not already the case. Adele wondered if she was looking at the core staffing of a presidential campaign.

Though Brockhurst was a long shot possibility for the nomination, stranger things than his emerging as a contender had happened in presidential politics. The prospects of dark horses were no doubt stimulated beyond normal because the two-term president was ineligible to run. The number of potential contenders in Brockhurst's party, which had not held the White House in a dozen years, were numerous. They all shared the characteristics of limited funding, similar qualifications and the absence of any distinguishing issue to separate one from the other.

Adele had only waited a few minutes when she was invited into the senator's office with abundant courtesy and amiability, which suited a political staff on the make with the media, Adele reflected with a tad of cynicism. Immediately inside the door to the senator's office, the tall, gray haired figure came forward from behind the massive desk to greet her. His right hand stretched forward to shake her hand, the face familiar from numerous press conferences and newspaper photos smiled broadly as he said, "Mrs. Friedman, pleased you could come today." Adele was surprised that Brockhurst addressed her with a title other than the generic Ms. which she routinely used. He or his staff had done sufficient research to know she was or had been married. She was not normally the object of such preparation by someone she was about to interview.

Adele distractedly grasped the offered hand and thanked Brockhurst for taking the time to give her an interview. Despite her attendance at many of the senator's press conferences, Adele was surprised to find that Brockhurst was an even more imposing figure up close. He stood several inches over six feet. Age had not thickened his waist very much and the broad shoulders allowed his coat to hang in a fashion that would have done credit to a younger, trimmer man. Adele wondered if such a physical appearance added some additional motivation to a man's succumbing to the lure of presidential aspirations. Did looking the part nourish an interest in the possibility of being president? Adele was enough of a believer in the power of imagery to think, in a certain kind of personality, a dominating appearance might make one think high office more attainable.

Brockhurst turned to a man who was standing across the room behind a high back chair and said, "Let me introduce a key member of my staff, Harold Fortner." Adele could not place the name immediately as the man moved toward her rapidly. He was a man of medium height. His well-cut suit covered a trim body. His face was youthful and made estimating his age difficult, perhaps belying his years. Somehow, he exuded aggressiveness without any overt gesture and before uttering a word.

"Ms. Friedman, pleased to meet you," he said. Adele managed a smile though she was distracted by her failure to recall why Fortner's name was familiar. She was sure she knew the names of all the senator's senior staff, and Fortner's was not among those people. "You look puzzled, Ms. Friedman," Fortner said. "Should we enlighten the lady, senator?" said Fortner as he turned to Brockhurst.

"I think that we can count of Mrs. Friedman's professionalism to respect off-the-record information," said Brockhurst, smiling at Adele. He fixed Adele with his most earnest and candid expression. "Hal is helping me to explore the possibility of pursuing my party's presidential nomination. He is experienced at testing the waters, so to speak. So I will rely on him to help me make the decision that it is or is not realistic to announce for the nomination. I'd like to avoid one of those brief, hopeless and expensive attempts that is doomed before it begins."

"There's nothing mysterious about what I do, Ms. Friedman," Fortner injected. "The senator has the record, the values and the ability to hold the office, but that all means nothing if the money and the potential for broad-based support isn't likely. We'll look at the possibilities for financing, the chances for delegate support, the issues that concern the voters; basic stuff that leads to an assessment that a campaign is or isn't plausible."

Adele now placed Fortner. He was a professional campaign consultant. He had run several successful gubernatorial and senate campaigns around the country and had even been involved in more than one presidential campaign. Adele did not know much about him but the little she did know was not flattering. He had a reputation for counter-productive aggressiveness and too much agility in switching clients. His abrasiveness and shiftiness would make his unemployable in political campaign management except for a preponderant ratio of successes over failures. However, Fortner did not always leave amiability in his wake. He had left several campaigns abruptly when he felt that his recommended courses of action had been challenged or not adopted with alacrity.

"Of course I know of Mr. Fortner by reputation, senator. Also, I understand your unwillingness to announce unless conditions are favorable for a realistic effort. You can count on my treating Mr. Fortner's involvement off the record at this stage. I hope, of course, that you won't forget me when the time comes for you to make an announcement," Adele offered agreeably.

The reporter in her saw an irresistible opening. "Would you be willing today to answer some follow-up questions to Abe Fuller's recent column regarding your vote against the bill barring public funding of pro sports stadiums?"

"If we stick to that specifically," leveled the senator. He gestured toward a chair by way of invitation. Adele sat and opened a note pad while the senator took a seat opposite her. Fortner moved out of Adele's line of sight. She imagined that he meant to offer signals to his client without Adele's observing it.

"Don't you agree that some cities have seriously over-committed themselves financially to attract to or keep professional teams in town by funding stadium projects, which, after all, are for the benefit of a profit-making entity?" Adele asked.

"In a few places, I think the evidence of that over-commitment is manifest, but I do think that the decision to make such a commitment is a matter for the exercise of good sense at the local level. There never was a better guide for financial decisions that the simple rule 'if you can't afford it, don't do it.' A city ought to be free to make that judgment itself rather than being prohibited from considering wholly or partially funding a stadium at public expense. After all, it's usually a bonding decision, not the immediate handover of millions of dollars."

"Of course, bonding for any expense moves a city toward the limit of its ability to sell bonds. Therefore, other needs may have to be delayed until the stadium bonds are retired," Adele pointed out.

"Quite true," Brockhurst said with an approving nod. "Assessing local circumstances is always the key. This city's decision to fund a stadium for the new pro football team after careful consideration of the city's present and future borrowing needs--"

"Excuse me, senator," Adele heard Harold Fortner's voice from directly behind her chair. "I think that your last point beings us to the point of receiving from Ms. Friedman the data that her paper said that it would provide."

Senator Brockhurst said nothing but raised his eyebrows quizzically at Adele. "Of course," she said and leaned down to extract an envelope from her handbag. She handed it to the senator, who tore the envelope open and began to examine the sheets he removed. Fortner moved around to read over his employer's shoulder.

Adele waited a few minutes and began to explain, since the data were not accompanied by any analysis. "There are two kinds of reaction there. One aggregate is the unsolicited reactions which readers are prompted to e-mail to our web site or sent through U.S. mail. The other data summary is the results of a survey of a carefully designed demographic sample of the region's population constructed by such factors as age, income level, educational level and several other factors."

"Would party affiliation be one of those other factors?" the senator asked with raised eyebrows.

"No, but a self-assignment on a scale with liberal or conservative as the opposite ends is included if the respondent is willing to give it," said Adele. "As with the random feed back, the comments from the sample are probably more meaningful to you than the summary rating. As you can see, Fuller's article was favorably judged, having received a summary rating of 4 on a 5 point scale. But there is no way to tell if it is the viewpoint of the columnist or your vote on the stadium bill that they approved of."

Harold Fortner smiled. "All the comments from both sources support your position on the public funding of sports stadiums, senator. I think that's the important thing," emphasized the political consultant with obvious satisfaction.

"Of course, no one expressed opposition to the bill which would prevent using public money," Adele injected demurely.

"Or supported it, either," Fortner pointed out. "They know your vote assured them a state of the art stadium for their new pro football team. It's a confirmation that, while the state and its one major population center are not among the largest in numbers, the state of North Louisiana and Pauliapolis are a part of the big time mainstream in America. That's important to them, as it is to people in all the major league sports cities of the country."

"Do you really think people get their status from that--from having big-time pro sports in town?" Adele asked, though she had long since been saddened by concluding that the answer was a resounding yes.

"People not only derive their status from having professional sports in their city or region, but really feel proud and successful if it's a winning pro team," said Fortner. "And a championship team has them in ecstasy about everything in general. The senator has given a tremendous boost to this state through his active support of the effort to get the expansion team for which this city was the long shot among four competitors. Its given him a wealth of political capital that should get him a favorite son commitment from the state's delegates to the convention. It might be just the impetus to move an admittedly dark horse effort into serious consideration in other state primaries."

Senator Brockhurst looked a little uncomfortable with Fortner's rosy scenario. "Well, Mrs. Friedman, you see the kind of vision and drive that has made Harold one of the most sought after campaign consultants in the nation. I hope that he is on the right track about where I should be positioning myself, of course."

"It sounds like a very plausible approach," Adele said. "And the position that you took on the stadium financing bill seems pragmatically chosen in two respects. Building a new stadium for the Loggers, which seems impossible without public funding, is extremely popular in the state. Furthermore, to retain as a local decision the option to fund stadiums publicly is exactly in line with the prevailing position within your party on preferring state or local control over federal regulation."

The senator smiled at the reporter's grasp of the pragmatism of his actions. "I hope that you recognize that I was motivated as much by commitment to the principle of local control as well as the furtherance of my own interests."

"Isn't it delightful when the two go hand in hand?" Adele smiled. The senator permitted himself a brief chuckle.

"Senator," Fortner began from his position behind Adele's chair, "if Ms. Friedman has no other questions, I wonder if I might explore a matter with her?"

Brockhurst looked at Adele inquiringly. "Of Course," Adele offered and turned in her chair as the campaign consultant moved around it to face her.

"What can you tell us about this man Fuller who wrote the column?" Fortner asked.

"I don't understand what you mean," Adele responded, not as much puzzled as she was wary.

"It's unusual for a sports reporter and columnist to dabble in political writing, isn't it?" asked Fortner.

"As you pointed out earlier, Mr. Fortner," Adele responded, "in our country, people's interest in the two matters is intertwined. Hence, a journalist who writes about one is always sensitive to the impingement of the other. The people react to the gains and losses of their political party in the same way that they do the wins and loses of their favorite team. Coming out on top seems to be as important to people in their allegiance to a sports team as much as to their political party. A good journalist takes that reality into account."

"And you think that explains why a sports writer strayed into political writing in this instance?" Fortner said, his face registering his lack of conviction.

Adele would have been comfortable to take responsibility for her own writing; however she realized that she could not admit her authorship of the column that was Fortner's concern.

"I think that it speaks well of Abe Fuller that he writes on meaningful topics rather than limiting himself to the superficial topics that most sports columns treat." She said this unabashedly because she was well satisfied with what Abe had written under her byline. Though it was not her style to admit it to Fuller, she had admired the substantive quality of his work ever since she had joined the Sentinel.

"I can't share your admiration," stressed Fortner. "The column was unnecessarily adversarial to try to make the senator look bad at such a sensitive time. I think we ought to know what axe he has to grind. What's his game? Is he some kind of radical or something?"

"I wouldn't have any idea of his politics and I don't think that you ought to be asking."

"I'm sure that Harold doesn't mean to be adversarial, Mrs. Friedman," Senator Brockhurst hastened to inject. "In his desire to fulfill the assignment I've hired him for, he is naturally concerned with the stance of the media. He has no desire that either you or Mr. Fuller will be offended. Is that not so, Harold?"

"Absolutely," Fortner stressed. "We'd be fools to offend the press. I'm just concerned that we get a fair shake. That the senator's record not be misconstrued is my only concern."

"Speaking for both the writer of that column and me, I think that I can assure you of that," Adele said and rose from her chair. She sensed that it was time to get off the ice before it cracked under her feet. Besides, she concluded that it was time to explore the background of Harold Fortner extensively rather than continue the insubstantial minuet that she was enduring. Adele had grown as interested in him as he seemed to be about the person whom he thought had written the column that had annoyed him.

Adele was profuse in expressing her thanks for the interview. She was thankful that she had not been obligated by her editor to actually do a story. However, she thought she laid the groundwork for something innocuous should she be obliged to write something, She confirmed with the senator that it would be acceptable if she reported him as favoring local control on the matter of public funding of pro sports facilities. If pressed she could do an acceptable non-news news item on that subject. With that basis of amiability now well-established she left the senator's office.

Chapter

8

Adele mulled at some length whether or not she should give Abe an account of her interview with Senator Brockhurst. She would take some satisfaction in telling him that the only meaningful content in the session was off the record, as she had predicted. The competitive journalist in her decided not to reveal what the meaningful story was that she could eventually write should Brockhurst run for president and continue to use Fortner to guide his effort. However, her conscience nagged her that Abe ought to know about the hostile attitude of Harold Fortner toward him for something he had not even written. Finally she decided that Abe ought to know there was the potential for hostility toward him from Brockhurst's office even though she need not be specific in naming anyone in particular as the likely source of that animosity. Abe deserved to know that any difficulty that befell him came from something Adele had written rather than from something Abe had produced himself.

She went to Abe's cubicle, part of her hoping that he would not be there. She was not delighted to find that he was. She seated herself beside his desk. It would have been helpful if he had spoken, but he simply looked at her with curiosity. "I'm delighted to see you too," she said with a touch of sarcasm when the silence and his scrutiny of her became uncomfortable.

"I'm simply overwhelmed at the honor," Abe said, reflecting her tone. "In the two years you've worked here, you've never stopped by before."

Adele was about to continue the barbed exchanges when she caught herself short. She wondered for a moment why all her dialogue with Abe Fuller had an edge to it, then decided she could not deviate from the established pattern now. "Yeh, well you can put up a plaque later. I have to tell you something."

"That seems always to be the case."

"Try to be serious for a moment," Adele urged. "I have to tell you something about my interview with Brockhurst." Passing over Brockhurst's rationale for his committee vote, Adele focused on the presence of a member of the senator's staff and his evident hostility toward Abe. She told Abe that the staffer in question believed that Abe had slanted his column to inject controversy into the senator's reasonable vote on the proposed bill prohibiting public funding for pro sports stadiums.

Abe shrugged his shoulders and said, "Doesn't sound to me like anything to be concerned with."

"This guy's considered a heavyweight member of the senator's staff, Abe," Adele stressed. "I don't want you to get blind-sided for a column that you didn't even write. A column, by the way, that I honestly thought was harmless."

"So he is annoyed that his boss's views may be a little harder to sell in the halls of congress than he would like. That's his problem," Abe asserted dismissively. "It was a good column that made a reasonable point. I'm fine with standing behind it."

"You're not concerned that Brockhurst could make trouble for you here in Pauliapolis?" Adele asked.

"If it comes from the column you wrote for my byline, so be it. I'm jealous you found that information before I did or I'd have written the column myself." Abe's face blossomed into a grin as he added, "Perhaps more stylishly, of course."

"Etheridge is a big supporter of Brockhurst's. Surely you don't believe the myth that newspaper owners never chastise their writers or fire them for what they've written?"

"Actually I know from experience that they do," Abe said ruefully. "But that column doesn't make Brockhurst look bad. Kind of makes him look good to the home folks, which is where all dark horse presidential candidacies have to start, don't they?"

"You're not annoyed that, if there is any trouble, that you didn't make it for yourself?" Adele was surprised at Abe's equanimity.

"No," Abe nodded. "I'll just write something for your byline that will make your life hell. Or are you going to chicken out of the last column we are to write for each other? I figure we're about even after the three so far. This next one tells the tale."

"Maybe we ought to call it off," Adele suggested.

"I was just kidding about writing a piece that would bite you," Abe assured. "Or are you thinking that sending me to the Caribbean is too expensive for your budget?" Abe grinned challengingly.

"Don't get carried away, Fuller," Adele snapped. "I was just trying to let you know where you stand. As far as our little competition, I'm already looking into first class flights and deluxe accommodations. You had better stock up on canned goods so that you won't starve while I'm lying in the sun."

"Oh, I'll stock up all right, and I'll leave it where you can get at it while I'm away." He leaned back in his chair and exuded as much confidence as he could bring to the surface, which was more than he actually felt.

As Adele readied herself to go, she offered, "You know, I wasn't going to tell people who's paying for my winter vacation, but if you keep displaying that attitude, I'm going to have to subject you to public embarrassment."

"Or, you could try talking me into a non-disclosure agreement," Abe smiled at the back of his exiting colleague. He wondered why he had not noticed Friedman's very attractive, lithe body before. He was either getting old or was becoming more intensely devoted to his work. He hoped it was the latter, he didn't want to think he was beyond being interested in the opposite sex, not that he wanted to get interested in Adele Friedman. He liked Adele but she had a sense of independence that it would be a fulltime occupation to breech successfully.

Abe had been sincere in his belief expressed to Adele that Brockhurst could not make serious trouble for him. However, he did not doubt that, should he write anything that damaged Senator Brockhurst's budding presidential hopes, no matter how defensible, the piece would result in chastisement by the paper's owner delivered through the editorial staff.

Abe always chuckled inwardly at letters to the editor that attributed widespread bias among reporters against free enterprise or other conservative verities. Such people imagined that newspaper owners, most of whom were political conservatives, were so tolerance of opposition to the conservative political philosophy that they held dear that they would continue to employ any journalist who was blatantly prejudiced against their views. Still, Abe had to admit that the abrupt removal of a journalist who occasionally discomforted the owner of a publication was an infrequent happening.

Thus, it was curiosity more than apprehension that led Abe to try to identify the member of Brockhurst's staff who was suspicious of him. He resolved not to devote much time to his inquiry, but at least a scrutiny of all stories emanating from the senator's office in the past year in which one of Brockhurst's staff was mentioned or had spoken on his behalf would be interesting. In a couple hours he found only the mention of staffers with whom his contacts had been uniformly innocuous.

Abe was about to conclude the effort when he decided to devote one more hour to it. He drove across town to the parking lot of the federal court house. He was certain that the senator had a reserved parking spot that carried his name. He wondered if there was anyone on the senator's staff who was also so privileged. That would at least tell him if there was a heavy hitter on the senator's staff that rated unusual privilege and was perhaps the one who had expressed his displeasure with Abe to Adele. A little cruise around the lot brought him to the senator's labeled space. Abe noted that there was an assigned space next to Brockhurst's, but the name was not one of those on the senator's list of occasional spokespersons. The name was totally unfamiliar to him. The person might not have any connection to the senator at all. It might be coincidence that it was next to Brockhurst's space; however, Abe jotted down the name Fortner. It was worth a google search.

When Abe found how extensively a political campaign consultant named Harold Fortner was mentioned in articles on the internet, he read as much of the man's self-aggrandizing facebook page as he could stand. It was safe to conclude that Senator Brockhurst had employed Fortner to explore the possibility of a presidential run. He was probably the person on the senator's staff who expressed doubts about Abe's objectivity toward the senator.

Having been away from political journalism for almost a decade, Abe excused himself for never having heard of Fortner. He focused on those articles which were devoted to Fortner himself rather than the candidates for whom he had worked. He was invariably discussed for the intensity with which he attacked his work as a political consultant. Having accepted a client, he became as determined or even more so than the candidate to win the election. If a candidate had not sharply defined some issues on which to campaign before Fortner came aboard, that focus was not lacking for long.

Occasionally the candidate's other supporters were not enthusiastic about the issues Fortner sold to the candidate. That invariably meant that someone, either Fortner or the doubting campaign workers, would leave the campaign. Fortner's impressive percentage of successful campaigns dictated that the candidate usually chose to adopt Fortner's campaign strategies. However, a candidate occasionally lost his popularity and the election because he or she came off as a public relations construction rather that his or her own person. Yet, a surprising number of aspiring politicians seemed willing to become what Fortner made of them as the price of gaining the career that they had developed a passion for. If Senator Brockhurst's interest in a presidential run became active, Adele would have an arduous task on behalf of her readers. She would have to continue to separate for them the well-known and popular Brockhurst from the Fortner modifications that were sure to come in trying to appeal to a national audience.

Chapter

9

be had not proceeded beyond assessing what public sources could tell him about Harold Fortner when he had to leave for that night's baseball game between the Pauliapolis Stags and the visiting team from Des Moines. The prospect of national league football in the city had not diminished interest in the city's minor league baseball team. Though Abe, as a columnist predominantly, was not directly responsible for writing the story of the game, he was a faithful spectator at Stag home games both because he liked baseball and because the Stags were a talented group of very young and very veteran players who always made for an interesting contest and frequent material for a column.

The evening's game was no exception to the Stags' usual enjoyable performance, Abe mused as he left the stadium. He walked toward his car as he recollected the Stags' ninth inning come-from-behind victory achieved through some daring base running rather than by the power hitting but erratic portion of their lineup. Deep in his thoughts, Abe was surprised when a car eased up beside him and a honeyed feminine voice offered, "I'll give you a lift to your car." Abe looked down at the smiling, beautiful face that looked up at him from the open driver's side window of a huge black Mercedes sedan.

Impulse rather than appraisal prompted Abe to say, "Thanks, but I'm parked right over there," pointing to his veteran compact that sat less than twenty yards away.

"So it won't be a long trip," said the still smiling stranger, whose striking blue eyes were impressive even in the dim light of the parking lot. "Come on," she directed with a toss of her long blonde hair toward the seat beside her. "Get in. This is not a come on; I need to ask you a question."

Abe could think of a variety of questions that might be asked by either of them at this point. None of them were likely to be about the just completed baseball game. However, he easily convinced himself that his professional curiosity demanded that he continue the encounter. As he slipped into the soft leather passenger seat of the big sedan, the woman turned slightly in her seat and revealed to Abe a bit more of her long, lovely legs. She extended a hand and said, "I'm Caroline."

"Abe Fuller," he responded as he gripped the soft, manicured hand.

"I know who you are," she said and accelerated the car slowly toward Abe's weathered compact. "I'm hoping you can help me with a little problem."

Abe grinned. "This is different. I'm usually the one wanting people to help me with my problems."

She flashed another smile in Abe's direction. "I'd like you to set up a meeting for me with Adele Friedman."

"You don't need my help with that," Abe said, "Just call her at the Sentinel. She's a very available. I'm sure she'd meet with you."

"I don't want to phone and have some receptionist ask for my name. I need this to be confidential," the woman said, not turning to face Abe as she stopped her car next to Abe's Focus. "I'd like you to set it up and keep it off the record. It might be worth your while."

"How could it be worth my while? You seem sure Friedman's the person you need."

"Look," the woman began earnestly, "I approached you because I knew where to find you, and I have no idea how to run into her quietly. You'll be doing the paper a big favor to set up my meeting with

Adele Friedman. That ought to do you some good." The beautiful face turned to Abe and offered a smile both radiant and mysterious.

"Why not just give your story to me?" Abe suggested.

"A sports columnist?" she asked, her smile turning wry. "I don't think so."

Abe tried to look reassuring. "I can handle whatever story you've got. Besides, here you are at the ball park. That makes me think there might be a sports angle."

"It's a political story," the blonde said, turning suddenly more intense.

"I could bring Friedman in on it," Abe proposed. "It might have more impact covered from a couple of angles. There must be a reason you didn't approach Friedman directly."

"I could care less how the paper handles the story," she said dismissively. "My interest is in what I get for the story plus a firm promise of confidentiality."

"You mean you want to sell the story?" Abe asked, exhaling in surprise. "I can't remember if the paper ever paid for a story."

"Never?" asked the disbelieving blonde with raised eyebrows.

"Oh, I suppose the paper would pay for an exclusive on the second coming, but other than that, it's unlikely."

"How about a story that could affect the presidential election?" came the woman's cool question.

Abe tried not to show his doubts. In his experience, people generally over-estimated the impact of the stories that they offered to journalists, whether they were motivated by animus, public-spiritedness or greed. In fact, those motivated by the prospect of personal gain tended to inflate the sensational value of their stories the most.

"So basically, you want to talk to Adele Friedman to see if she'll carry your offer to sell a story to the paper's management for you?" Abe asked. To the woman's affirmative nod, Abe continued, "I can tell you what she's going to say. She'll want to know some specifics about the story to decide whether taking it to the editor is worth the effort."

"Obviously I'm not going to be very specific before payment is delivered," the woman said with a smile that suggested the intriguing nature of what she had to tell.

"I can tell you right now that what you've hinted isn't going to tempt the paper to buy the story," Abe said candidly. "Why don't you tell me a little about the story, and I'll judge for myself if the paper would be interested in buying it."

The woman laughed. "I do work at preserving my youth, but I didn't think that I looked like I was born yesterday. If you want to deal for me, I'll tell you this much. It's the political story of the decade for this state, and it will generate considerable national coverage."

"You think that this much specificity is going to convince the paper to pay for the whole story, in your not-so-expert judgment?" Abe countered.

"You do know the old maxim 'sex sells'?" the blonde offered demurely. "That's all you get. Run it up the line or not, I can live with it either way."

"Not that I'm committed to taking this to the paper for you, but do you have a figure in mind regarding what this story is worth?" Abe asked.

"Twenty-five thousand to hear the story and fifty more if you print it."

"Really?" Abe responded with a little gasp as he pressed back against his seat in surprise. "Not pricing yourself out of the market, are you?"

The blonde looked at Abe coolly. "Cheap under the circumstances. If things develop as they might, there'll be a bidding war to talk to me, and triple the seventy-five will be needed just to get an interview with me."

Abe pondered whether the woman ought to be taken seriously. Extreme expectations from sources insisting on confidentiality most likely came from delusional people. However, the investment of time and risk were minimal for him. "Give me a number where I can get in touch with you," Abe asked.

"I'll look you up in a day or two," she said, all business now.

That was Abe's cue to exit. He stood behind the big sedan as it cruised away. The car's license plate was clearly visible. He wrote it down and decided to check it out before he bothered to speak to Adele and Henry Burton about buying a story.

The next morning, what he discovered from coaxing some information from sources at the department of motor vehicle registration lacked the specificity to take something firm to her colleagues as a basis for buying a supposedly sensational story. The Mercedes was leased from a local dealer. However, the lessee was not an individual but a company called Xanadu. Obviously the lady who called herself Caroline did not care to be readily known. What profession, Abe asked himself, might an anonymous beautiful lady be in who had a story to sell that involved sex and politics? The list of obvious possibilities was quite short, and it did not need a veteran newspaper man to reach the likely conclusion. Well, at least he had an interesting speculation to take to his colleagues at the Sentinel, Abe concluded.

Chapter

10

Adele had trouble keeping her mind on her efforts to probe the background of Harold Fortner. After the abrasive exchange she and Abe had had over his having recommended that she be assigned the interview with Senator Brockhurst, she wondered if Abe Fuller intended that they would finish their writing contest or if his annoyance was sufficient to his dropping the matter. She had lectured herself that she ought not to care if his petulance caused a rift between them. Yet she preferred that there not to be a rift. She actually enjoyed his thorniness and would prefer that they be friends. Still she was irritated that her dwelling on Abe's mood distracted her from her work.

The ringing of her phone brought her out of her reverie. Her greeting her caller with her last name was responded to with a dramatic gasp of astonishment. "Is it really? Really the honest-to-heaven Adele Friedman, the jazziest journalist in the Midwest?"

"Hey, Fitzie, Thanks for returning my call," Adele responded pleasantly.

"You're going to get business-like on me?" shot back Katherine Fitzwalter, a reporter for the Washington Sun, who had been a friend of Adele's since they were contemporaries in journalism school. "You don't call me for six months and you get business-like on me when I return your call?"

"Aw, Fitz, you know how it is," Adele pleaded.

"Actually I don't, but let me speculate. You have a fantastic lover who keeps you tied to his bed for days on end. Or, you're working undercover on a story about federal prisons by getting yourself convicted of a felony, or, you've left journalism and have been living on an island in the middle of a North Louisiana lake while you write a thousand page novel. It better be one of those or I have no idea why you haven't been in touch for six months."

"Well, Fitz," Adele offered with as much honey as she could muster for a rationalization, "I didn't want to intrude on your involvement in the engrossing panorama which is the nation's capital."

"Right," Fitzwalter groused, "like I'm in daily contact with the powerful and the super-powerful."

"Hey," Adele injected, "I've seen the syndication of lots of your stories. Good stuff, Fitzie."

"Back at you," came the voice to Adele. "I've seen a couple interesting columns of yours lately."

"Yeh, well that's another story I'll tell you about sometime," Adele entered pointedly. "Listen, Fitz, I need some information."

"Why else would you be calling, Adele? Not to find out if your old roommate is well or fatally ill."

"Are you fatally ill?" Adele asked.

"Not today. That was last week," said Fitzwalter. "What is it that you want to know?"

"The political consultant Harold Fortner has his home base in your unfair city, doesn't he?" Adele asked.

"Ah, the smarmy Svengali of political campaigning," Fitzwalter said sarcastically. "Yes, he does. What's he up to now?"

"Did you know that he's working on Senator Randall Brockhurst's possible run for his party's presidential nomination?" Adele asked.

"It's well known and something of a puzzle. Brockhurst is a long shot possibility, and Fortner's reputation is such that some people are surprised that Fortner hasn't hooked up with a more visible possibility."

"Since the incumbent President isn't running," Adele began

hesitantly, aware that she was unlikely to make any analysis that her expert friend had not already considered, "Isn't it the case that even possibilities from sparsely populated states have a shot at this stage? Besides, Brockhurst's party could do a lot worse than him, and probably will."

"You said the key phrase, which is 'at this stage,' Adele," Fitzwalter responded, with the tone of one professional to another. "You know as well as I that the first weeding in a presidential campaign is to eliminate those who can't afford to run. Brockhurst falls into that category. Hence the puzzlement that Fortner hooked up with him. Brockhurst doesn't figure to have very deep pockets, either of his own or from donors."

"Maybe Fortner didn't have any choice," Adele speculated.

"Oh, Adele, you can't be serious. Fortner's track record of successes is such that he can pick his horse to ride."

"Below the presidential level, he has brought a couple of real long shots into the winner's circle," Adele mused. "Maybe he sees Brockhurst as actually having a chance."

"Word has it that Fortner has already passed on a couple of likely campaigns that appear to have as much of a chance politically as Brockhurst's and have a lot more money; I mean a lot," Fitzwalter emphasized.

"If want you say is true," Adele sighed, "I can't imagine what his reason would be."

"My guess," Fitzwalter began, "is that it's the oldest reason in the world. You think that I had no reason to call him 'smarmy'?"

"I can never get it straight," Adele admitted. "Is the oldest reason in the world greed or sex?"

"Really, Addie, I think you have been in the Midwest too long. There's little doubt that Fortner would say 'sex.' Look for the presence of some real babe on Brockhurst's staff and you'll know why Harold Fortner is in Pauliapolis for the earliest stage of a presidential campaign--the stage where there is still time to pursue the basics of life. That would square with his reputation in this town."

"You can't believe that he'd pass up a major candidate's campaign for a crazy reason like that," Adele gasped. "Nobody has that much trouble keeping his pants zipped."

"Try that theory out on his three ex-wives," Fitzwalter chuckled. "Look; it's not time for the main event. He has plenty of time to get another horse if Brockhurst falters in the early running," Fitzwalter offered confidently.

"Maybe," admitted Adele dubiously. That non-committal word was as far as she could go toward agreeing with her friend's perception.

"So nose around a bit," Fitzwalter suggested. "I'll expect your call telling me I was right."

"More likely, I'll be chiding you for having become too cynical in the corrosive atmosphere of the nation's capital," Adele asserted. "There are limits to what people will risk for sex."

"Did you sleep through the Clinton administration, Addie?" Fitzwalter asked. "Call me," she added before she broke off.

Adele wished her friend goodbye and hung up. She studied the phone for some time after she hung up.. She knew from long experience that Fitzwalter was not a cynic who reduced all human behavior to some simple, negative explanation. Most likely she had Fortner pegged right. Of course, there was another possibility. Maybe Brockhurst had more campaign financing than would be usual for a long-shot candidate from a sparsely populated state. Maybe Harold Fortner was working for the Brockhurst campaign because the senator could make a serious run for the nomination. The possibility was worth at least a cursory look.

Chapter

After Abe failed to identify the woman who wanted to sell the Sentinel what she claimed to be a sensational political story with national appeal, he tried to learn her identity by describing her to people who were purported to know the most expensive and discrete playmates in the city. This failed to produce a name either, probably because Abe was unconvincing as a potential client and the sources had no interest in disturbing a fundamental part of the local economy.

Still, he thought it wise to take the matter to Henry Burton framed in the context of his speculations. As concisely as he could, he told Burton that he had been approached by a seemingly-affluent and beautiful woman that he suspected was a local call girl who wanted to sell the paper a scandalous story with national political implications.

Henry Burton's facial expression looked to be a combination of doubt and boredom. "What was the lady's name?"

"Caroline. Caroline was all she gave," Abe said.

"How surprising," Burton murmured, looking even less interested than before. "Nothing else stirs the blood of a newspaper editor like an anonymous source who wants to be paid for a vague story that's supposed to be political dynamite."

"She said the story was about sex," Abe stated.

"Another shock," sighed Burton. "How much does the lady want for this undisclosed bombshell?"

"Twenty-five thousand dollars, to hear it; fifty more if we run it," reported Abe.

"I doubt the lady's entire client list would be worth twenty-five thousand dollars, if she included color photos," Burton scoffed.

Abe smiled as he spotted an opening. "I see you inferred as I did that she is the plaything of a prominent politician. Maybe not. She may just have a rumor about someone who is a client of one of her competitors."

Burton shrugged his shoulders, "Maybe she wants twenty-five thousand just for a rumor for us to follow up."

"With a little leg work the rumor might lead us to somebody big, like Senator Brockhurst. Why else would she hint at an impact on the presidential campaign?" Abe said with more conviction than he actually felt.

"Have you considered that the truth is that she wants twenty-five thousand dollars and--" Burton paused for emphasis, "exaggeration is the best way to get it?" offered Burton.

Burton donned his schoolmaster's expression. "If the story would turn out to have any truth, it would probably be about a first term state legislator from the boondocks who has just discovered the delights of the big city that are not readily available back home."

"And so we'd have invested twenty-five thousand in a story that we normally would run on the inside pages of the second section," Abe admitted. "But what if it turns out to be the other possibility? A presidential hopeful with a sterling, family-man image has a major character problem."

Burton shook his head thoughtfully. "I don't know. You're asking me to go to Etheridge with a request to spend a lot of money on a pig in a poke. Besides, he and Brockhurst are close personal friends. He might not want to run the story even if it's true."

"Come on, Henry, it can't hurt just to talk to him. Besides he might want to know before he backs a lame horse for president."

Henry Burton looked deep in thought for a minute. "I want to talk to someone first." He picked up his phone and punched some numbers. "Burton here. Can you come up here now?" he said to the respondent.

Abe had no idea who might appear in response to the summons and sat in silence until the door opened and Adele Friedman entered the editor's office. Adele frowned at Abe but said nothing. Burton offered her a seat and said that he wanted her reaction to a story that Abe had brought to him. He nodded to Abe to present the matter.

Abe recounted his experience of last evening and the speculations that had flowed from it. Adele, shook her head and said conclusively, "If it's anything more than fiction, it couldn't be about Brockhurst."

Abe was amused at the definitive air of Adele's assertion. "How can you be so sure of that?"

Adele returned Abe's smile. "After that delightful but insubstantial interview that I did with the senator and the campaign consultant for his as yet unannounced run for his party's presidential nomination, I decided to look into the background of Harold Fortner, the campaign consultant. If the story is about what it appears to be, the lady's client who's involved in politics is Fortner, not the senator."

"What leads you to that conclusion," asked Henry Burton, barely getting his question in before Abe could react.

"Apparently Fortner has a well-established reputation as a womanizer," Adele explained.

"Well-established with whom?" Abe responded dubiously.

"My source is very reliable," Adele said confidently. "I think that confirmation would be easy to get if the story's worth pursuing. I doubt the story's worth some preliminary scrutiny, let alone the money."

"I think the story has some interest, even if it is about Fortner. He's a major player in the campaigning industry. Wasn't he involved in the president's re-election campaign four years ago?"

Both Adele and Burton nodded affirmatively. "Well, then," Abe argued, "isn't there some reader interest in exposing the hypocrisy of someone who was involved in that nauseating family values campaign of four years ago?"

Henry Burton tightened his jaw as he did when an idea piqued his interest minimally but left him unconvinced of its worthiness.

Adele broke the brief silence. "You'd pay twenty-five thousand for that story?"

"Let me try to negotiate the figure downward, Henry," Abe suggested.

Henry Burton pondered silently for a minute before he sighed. "The owner wouldn't be pleased with any story that even peripherally damages his old friend Senator Brockhurst."

"Better to give Brockhurst a reason to dump the man now than to have him be a major problem later, Henry. We'd be doing the owner's friend a favor," Abe emphasized.

Adele let a chuckle escape her pursed lips. "What a spinmeister you are, Fuller. Maybe you ought to go into campaign consulting."

Burton's expression became the one that invariably showed when he gave a reporter an assignment that he expected to be pursued expeditiously and without challenge. "See if the lady will take five thousand for the full, and I do mean full, story. We probably won't get to use the story but Etheridge will probably think that much well-spent to save his friend any embarrassment."

"Henry, if we buy a story we expect never to print," Abe began with his distaste echoing through his tone, "doesn't that make us agents of the Brockhurst campaign?"

"We can't be certain that the story would never run regardless of the owner's connection to the senator," Burton said with little conviction. "Just do it."

When Abe and Adele had closed the door to Burton's office behind them, Adele smiled broadly and said, "So, Fuller, is this mystery lady something of a babe?"

"I don't notice things like that, Friedman. I'm a professional; it's the story that attracts my attention."

Adele over-dramatized her disbelief. "You are either a case of premature aging or an appalling liar."

"Perhaps a general impression of her appearance did register," Abe said with elaborate pretense of casualness. "I'd say she more of the swim suit model body type than the lingerie model type. Natural long blonde hair, flawless complexion, surprisingly rather innocent smile and--"

"Please don't go on with the things you didn't notice. I've just had lunch and I may grow ill," Adele interrupted.

"You did ask," Abe said with satisfaction.

"My question was just an attempt at small talk, which your response reduced to exceedingly small. I was leading up to what's really on my mind," Adele asserted a bit acerbically.

"We seem to be stuck on small subjects," Abe said with his own touch of annoyance. "What's on your mind?"

"Under the circumstances, is our little contest still on?" Adele asked.

"I don't see why not," Abe said flatly, "unless you want to cancel."

"I was only considering it as a favor to you," Adele said. In response to Abe's openmouthed look of surprise, she continued. "It's logical that Henry would expect my column for tomorrow to be on my interview with Brockhurst. Obviously you can't write that since you didn't do the interview."

Abe scoffed. "You think not? How's this? Since he's not ready to announce, he wants his interest in the nomination represented as merely exploratory. To make a decent column of it will necessitate putting his interest in the context of the national dynamics of an election where there is not an incumbent and no popular frontrunner in either of the major parties."

Adele's silence indicated that Abe was not far off from the likely content of the column. She said coolly, "I'd be doing you a favor to have you write such a bland column under my byline. It would give me the opportunity to write something for the column under your name with some content that would give me the contest. Unless, of course, I'd deliberately write a bad column to keep you from winning."

"I know Henry well enough to know that he wouldn't insist on a column about a nothing interview. I'll come up with something better than that. What wrong? Already out of ideas?"

"I do hope you'll live to an over-ripe old age, Fuller, but you won't live long enough to see me out of ideas," said Adele as she walked away.

Abe smiled at the departing figure, but felt somewhat less confident than his smile suggested.

Chapter

12

While Abe was puzzling over what would be his final column for Adele's signature, he was distracted by wondering when a phone call would come from his mystery woman. Between his clockwatching, Abe mentally rehearsed what he would say to the beautiful blonde if she did call. What wording could he use that would make a five thousand dollar payment be a reasonable amount for her entire story? He had trouble focusing on that question because he was still stumped for a good column subject. Abe was still without an alternative to the prosaic topic of writing for Adele's signature an account of her circumscribed interview with Senator Brockhurst. He was still puzzling over the last of the opening sentences he had tried that had led nowhere toward a subject that had even a remote chance of engaging his readers when his phone rang.

In response to his greeting the caller with his name, the woman identified herself as the lady who had given him a ride to his car last night. Attempting to convey enthusiasm he did not feel, Abe began, "I'm glad you called. I have good news."

Before Abe could continue, the caller said, "I really don't want to do this over the phone."

"What do you suggest?" Abe asked agreeably. She proposed that

Abe meet her on the top level of the parking garage attached to the city's most prominent department store in an hour. Abe agreed.

Fifty minutes later he standing near the entrance of the walkway from the garage into the store as arranged. A ten minute wait had just about convinced him that she would not show when the same black Mercedes that had pulled up to him in the previous night came into view from the ramp ascending to this topmost parking level. As the big black sedan stopped at his feet he saw that the blonde who was driving looked even more stunning in the daylight than she had in the dimly lit stadium parking lot. The woman motioned for Abe to get into the front passenger seat.

"So what has the paper decided?" the woman asked without turning her classic profile to look at Abe. There were not spaces to pull into and she was apparently unconcerned about additional traffic arriving.

"I have an offer for you which was not easy to get, since you didn't give me much to take to the editor. Maybe it's not exactly what you wanted but nevertheless profitable for you for what is, from the paper's perspective, a pig in a poke."

"I think this is going to be a short conversation," said the velvety voiced blonde.

"No, hear me out," Abe responded earnestly. "I took your story, which you'll have to admit is very vague at this point, to my boss, the managing editor.. He asked me to speculate about what the story might be, and here's what I came up with. The state's senior U.S. Senator has hired a consultant to help him decide if he can make a run for the presidential nomination. My guess is that you've had some involvement with this man, which would be a story of some interest, in view of it having some connection to a long shot contender in the upcoming presidential campaign. The value to the paper of confidential confirmation and some details on that story is five thousand dollars tops."

The classic profile stared ahead for a lengthy pause before responding in a quite unruffled tone. "Your guesswork isn't totally off-base, Mr. Fuller. However, it doesn't get anywhere near to the real meat of the story. I quite agree that a story of a bit of sex by a peripheral political figure is hardly a story worth printing these days." She turned her head to look Abe in the eyes.

"Let me give you just this much. It's the pillow talk and not who is involved in the sex that's the juicy part of this story. I can give you the specifics of a major story. The paper should be able to confirm the who of the sex if there's any kind of real journalist among the staff of the paper. The substance of the pillow talk will be of national interest for more than the proverbial fifteen minutes. You tell your boss that what I'm asking is cheap for the story that I can give you. Believe me, there will be no bargaining. And, I'm not going to wait forever before I take this story elsewhere."

Abe raised his hands palm outward toward the woman in a calming gesture, which was unnecessary, since her stony facial expression had not altered. "Look, let me work on this, but you've got to let me know how I can reach you. Since you're rushing this thing, I can't wait until you decide to call me."

The woman pulled a slip of paper from a very expensive-looking cashmere coat and handed it to Abe. "I'll be at that number at five o'clock this afternoon." She nodded toward the car door, making clear that the meeting was over.

Abe got out of the car and watched as the beautiful blonde drove away. He realized that he had nothing more than an additional hint of a supposedly sensational but very expensive story to take back to Henry Burton. However, his fertile mind could build more inferences around that new hint. She had not said that she had any tape recordings, but it was intriguing to speculate that she might. When he met again with Burton and Adele in the editor's office he would be prepared to state at least one and perhaps more speculations. He had no time to lose if he was to get a meeting at the paper before the five o'clock deadline the woman had set.

Later, after he had finished the bare account of his meeting with the mystery woman, he looked at the unenthusiastic faces of his two listeners and launched into his guesses. "If the lady's client is Harold Fortner, he has apparently spilled something important to her when they were relaxing after more strenuous activity. It was most likely about the Brockhurst campaign, and I'm guessing there is audio tape."

"Of course," Adele began with raised eyebrows and a disinterested tone, "There is no Brockhurst campaign."

"You think Fortner's in North Louisiana for a fishing trip?" Abe retorted.

"That's as good a description as any," Adele smiled. "This additional tidbit still doesn't give enough to merit plunking down five figures for."

"The lady's not going to negotiate on price," Abe said.

"What a shame," Adele said with mock concern. "You've got no reason to meet with her again. And you were getting along so well."

Abe was about to respond sarcastically when Burton called a halt to the sniper fire with a gesture of his hand.

Burton glanced at his watch and mused aloud, "The only thing that is certain is that we don't even have enough to made good guesses from. But I wonder if this latest teaser would have any impact on Mr. Etheridge's thinking. I'll fill him in and get back to Abe on whether we're going to pass or walk a little farther into this bit of fog."

After they left Henry Burton's office, Adele turned to Abe as they waited for the elevator and asked, "So how are you betting? Is the publisher going to invest?"

Abe shrugged his shoulders. "Who knows? If it were up to me, I'd buy the story, nebulous as it has been to this point, just on the chance that it might turn out to be something exceptional."

"Of course, your curiosity seems to go beyond the story," Adele offered with a tight lipped smile. In response to Abe's puzzled expression, she continued. "You know, to help you to keep things strictly professional, I could handle any further meetings with the lady with the soft curves and the big car."

"You wouldn't want to be getting the inside track on the story, would you?" queried Abe suspiciously.

"No, no," Adele injected and gestured in protest. "I was just offering to keep you from temptation. Of course, I've seen no evidence that you're even capable of amorous feelings."

"Or maybe there isn't anyone around here that could arouse such feelings," protested Abe, suddenly finding himself defending his ability to feel less than exemplary urges.

"Right," Adele smiled and walked toward the stairwell, her movements speaking for themselves about her ample capacity to tempt.

Chapter

13

Abe settled himself back into the difficult task of producing a column for Adele's signature that might produce the kind of survey numbers that would give him a victory in the writing competition with Adele. Curiously, though he did not yet have the least idea of the subject of this stunning column, he was considering the wording of a magnanimous victory speech in which he let Adele off the hook regarding paying for his week in the Caribbean and would suggest that they make the trip together with each paying his own way. He was still working on the exact wording of this proposal when Henry Burton phoned. The editor said that he could call the mystery source at five that afternoon and commit to the twenty-five thousand dollar purchase price with the proviso that the amount would be a final payment and that the source was to tell all that she knew and provide any and all confirmation that she had by way of tape or written material.

Abe expressed his enthusiasm and some surprise. Burton explained that the owner now saw tracking down the story as a favor to his friend the senator. Believing that the story was not about his friend's behavior but concerned the actions of a staff member who would damage his friend's career, Etheridge was willing to spend the money to find out exactly what was being alleged.

Checking the time, Abe returned to his writing task with renewed energy. He wanted to finish the column before five o'clock so that he could devote himself to the new, mysterious, political story with fully focused attention. When five o'clock arrived he punched in the number that the beautiful mercenary source had given him. He grew impatient when the number of rings had passed a dozen or more. Finally he gave up and decided to wait a few minutes before trying again. He called at three or four minute intervals over the next half-hour and received no answer. Midway through the unsuccessful enterprise he wondered if he was jumbling the numbers and used exaggerated care in punching the sequence of numbers. The result was always same, a series of unanswered rings.

Surrendering on his effort to reach the mystery blonde, Abe began to punch Henry Burton's number to report the unexpected development. He stopped in mid-effort. He decided to talk to Adele and started toward her office at the other end of the floor.

He related the situation to Adele concisely. Adele, to Abe's relief, spared him both belittlement or sarcasm. She frowned thoughtfully. "Maybe she's just late," she offered. When Abe reacted with a doubtful expression, she continued. "Stands to reason that she wouldn't give you her home or cell phone number. Probably it's a pay phone number. Maybe she's late getting there." Abe nodded affirmatively. They tried the number a half-dozen times in the following hour before they resigned themselves to failure.

After a brief silence, Abe mumbled an obscenity too indistinctly for Adele to hear and reached for her phone to call Henry Burton. Adele put her hand over the cradled phone and asked what he intended.

When informed, she asked, "Why do that? Let's try to find her. We've got some very good news to give the lady. Or, if she's no longer interested, we can coax her to tell us why."

"Find her?" Abe mused aloud. "And just how do you propose we do that?"

"The parking valets at the most expensive and admired restaurants in the upscale part of downtown may remember her and her black Mercedes sedan. Perhaps she and an occasional client may have enjoyed a gourmet meal as a preliminary to strenuous exercise. We have your very thorough description of her and we—I mean you—can provide some financial stimulus to their memories."

Abe shook his head and said, "Talk about a long shot."

Adele was not deterred. "There isn't a very long list of the most sumptuous places. You said she's probably top of the line, so to speak."

Abe raised his eyebrows. "I'm impressed with your grasp of the workings of professional sin, Friedman."

"You know what they say about small town girls," Adele smiled.

"What's that?"

"If you don't know at your age, Fuller, you probably can't handle it."

"Well," Abe said, "my less extensive knowledge of such matters convinces me otherwise. Chances are, if the lady and a client dine, they'd do so at some place out of town," Abe asserted, adhering to the subject at hand because no tart retort occurred him.

"Apparently you haven't explored the upscale dining options on the outskirts of Pauliapolis very thoroughly," Adele argued. "Look, I know it's a long shot, but why not give it a try?" Adele grinned challengingly, "Unless you have an exciting evening planned."

Abe nodded his acquiescence. "I've spent evenings on a lot less entertaining activities." Then he smiled suddenly and added. "I've got another idea. Surely, the lady would serve only the very best booze at home. Assuming that she lives downtown, we could ask the downtown liquor stores about deliveries to upper end clientele for the very best scotch and champagne, that kind of thing."

Adele could not suppress a smile. "So you are not totally without some insight into how the upscale world of sin works. Is that knowledge based on experience or is it purely theoretical?"

"You must have an erroneous notion of my salary," Abe said dismissively. "My perception of these matters comes from my reading."

Adele looked at her watch. "We'd cover more ground if we worked separately. Why don't you do the liquor stores and I'll do the fine dining spots?"

Abe feigned astonishment. "What? You probably think I've never heard of Grosscup's," Abe retorted, naming the city's most admired restaurant.

Adele stood and reached for her coat. "I'm not surprised you've heard of Grosscup's. I just don't want you going to MacDonald's from there."

Abe, who had no real objection to Adele's division of the labor, sighed an exaggerated attempt to display injured feelings. He then left Adele's office to report the lack of developments to Burton and get his coat to begin his share of their task. "Say, mastermind," came her voice trailing him. "You do have your cell phone?"

"Yes," Abe answered, "do you have my number?"

"I've always had your number, Fuller," came the answer, confirming for Abe that their cooperating together had produced no change in the style with which Adele Friedman related to him.

Chapter

14

An examination of the yellow pages and a street map of downtown established for Abe that he had six possibilities to explore, three of which were surprisingly near each other. On the assumption that it was likely that his quarry would have her liquor purchases delivered rather than carry them home herself, Abe began by asking the lone clerk in the first store whether or not they delivered purchases. Having received an affirmative reply, Abe asked the brands and prices of the store's best scotches, bourbons, and champagne. The clerk stated several brands in each type of beverage of above average quality and price. However, even a less than ardent drinker such as Abe recognized that the brands named were not the very top of quality or luxury in price. Abe pressed the clerk as to whether he had mentioned their very best stock. The man examined Abe's attire and appearance closely before responding. When the clerk did answer, his sarcastic tone conveyed that he doubted that his questioner could afford even the level of expense for the brands had been indicated as the store's highest quality stock, let alone, anything more expensive. Sure that additional questioning of the clerk would be pointless, Abe nodded and left.

Abe's experience with the first liquor store was repeated at the second one. However, before he left the store, he paid twenty dollars for an answer to the question: what brands of scotch, bourbon and champagne would someone buy who was a dedicated liquor snob for whom money was no object. The prices of the unfamiliar brands stated in the answer took more than a few moments to absorb and reminded him that the rewards for keeping the public well-informed were indeed modest in comparison with the cost of luxuries that people with much more income could afford. However, now armed with this relevant information, Abe spent little time in the third store when the clerks admitted that they did not stock the prestige brands that Abe mentioned.

At his fourth stop, he was responded to with effusive courtesy by a clerk who assumed he was a buyer of the prestige brands that Abe inquired if they carried. The man's friendliness evaporated quickly when Abe admitted he was not a buyer but wanted some information. After stimulating the man's interest by placing two twenty dollar bills on the counter, Abe asked if the store had a regular customer from a swank residence nearby to which they delivered these high quality beverages

To the terse response that they had several, Abe described his mystery lady with the most extravagant details he could recollect and hinted obliquely that she might possibly be a party girl. The clerk inquired the reason for Abe's curiosity. The man's reluctance was overcome by adding three more twenties to the pair on the counter and admitting that he was a reporter on a story that would not involve the clerk or the store.

The clerk said that the description resembled a repeat customer named Penelope Dayton. It took several more twenties for him to remember that Penelope Dayton's orders were delivered to the Riverside Towers, a luxury residential high rise on the banks of the Louisiana river, which flowed through the length of Pauliapolis. Exiting the liquor store, Abe tried to call Adele's cell phone and got a 'no service' message. He suppressed the recurring urge to throw his phone across the street into the park before a moment of rationality prevailed, and he decided to call Adele at the Sentinel. Before he began to thumb in the number, his phone buzzed an incoming call.

In answer to his greeting, the caller said, "Abe, it's Adele; can you meet me at the Riverside Towers right away?"

"I was just about to call you and ask you the same thing," Abe said placidly.

"Really?"

Foregoing the temptation to indulge in banter, Abe said, "I'll be there in less than a half hour." He was relieved that he had been as successful as Adele in uncovering a lead to continue their pursuit of the story. He also could not help but be impressed with Adele's investigative skills. Had he been inclined to offer compliments, which was decidedly not his style, he would have told Adele Friedman that she was unfair to the rest of her journalistic colleagues to be so good looking and capable too. Very capable indeed, thought the hard-shelled journalist.

"She's probably intimidating to a lot of guys," Abe laughed and said to the frosty night air, "Good thing I'm not short of ego."

By the time a cab deposited him in the semi-circular drive at the entrance of the Riverside Towers, Adele was pacing back and forth, her coat collar turned up and her arms folded across her chest to preserve her body heat against the night chill. Her shoulder-length hair was lifted away from her neck by the wind where the red tam set at a rakish angle did not keep it anchored. The temperature was just low enough to give her cheeks a glow, Abe noted. She looked so appealing that Abe could not think of a single sarcastic thing to say. In fact, he had to check himself or he might have said something complementary.

As he approached, Adele hunched her shoulders against the cold and said, "I thought you'd never get here."

Abe glanced at his watch and said, "I said less than a half hour. It's been twenty minutes."

"Seems longer. It's the cold."

Abe chuckled. "God. A guy'd think you hadn't grown up in this climate."

"You've never heard me say I loved it," Adele asserted.

"What will you do when it really gets cold?"

"I'm planning on a sun and surf vacation," Adele said with a sly smile.

Abe substituted a dismissive noise for a retort and nodded toward the building. "Shall we go in and visit the lady?"

"I'd love to, but how do we find out which apartment?" Adele frowned. "All I came up with is this address, and it took some luck to get that out of the parking valet at the restaurant. If he hadn't gotten her a cab once and heard her give this address, I wouldn't even have the address."

Abe toyed with claiming superior investigative skill and suppressed any such claim. "The lady's name is Ms. Penelope Dayton, a fact I know because she has her booze delivered," Abe stated with satisfaction yet absent any tinge of gloating.

"So then," Adele smiled broadly, "let's call on the lady and offer her twenty-five thousand dollars for one of the more interesting chapters in what I'm sure is a very busy career."

"She might be busy."

Adele renewed her smile. "At the price we're offering, maybe she'll be willing to take a night off."

Abe returned Adele's smile, "Or at least delay the evening's labors." He offered a sweeping wave of an arm to invite Adele to precede him into the lobby of the hotel.

Adele strode across the terrazzo floor to the counter behind which sat a security guard who alternated glances between his desk top and the security monitors banked on his right.

"We're here to see Ms. Penelope Dayton," Adele announced confidently to the guard.

The round face that looked too jovial to inspire caution in a visitor shook his head from side to side and said, "No Penelope Dayton lives here."

Abe responded assertively, "You sure? Striking blonde, late twenties or early thirties at most? Drives a black, late model Mercedes?"

"Maybe we have the first name wrong. She also goes by 'Caroline,'" Adele offered.

"Nope."

Adele offered the man her most engaging smile. "You needn't worry that she'll be upset if you tell her we're here. We has some very good news for her. Just tell her it's Fuller and Friedman. She'll want to talk to us."

"I'm telling you," the man said emphatically, "she doesn't live here."

Adele and Abe glanced at one another as the same thought occurred to them. Abe asked, "You mean she doesn't live here now?"

"Maybe."

Abe got out his wallet and pulled out his remaining sixty dollars as he showed Adele the empty compartment. Laying the money on the counter in front of the security guard, Abe asked, "How recently did she move?"

The guard silently looked at the money as though it were some unfamiliar food he was reluctant to try. "Did I say she moved?"

Adele added several bills to what Abe had left and said, "You won't be making any trouble for her to tell us. We're going to put a lot of money in her pocket."

"That's hard to believe."

"Why?" Abe asked.

"Why would she move away suddenly if she was about to come into a lot of money?" asked the guard.

"She moved today?" Adele asked incredulously.

The guard studied the little stack of money for a moment. His hand darted out and captured the bills before he spoke.

"Movers came this afternoon. Cleaned out the place in less than two hours. She put her suitcases in the car and drove off right behind them."

"Did she say where she was going?" Abe asked.

"Nope."

Adele put several more twenties on the counter. "Maybe you heard the movers say where they were taking her stuff."

"I might have."

Adele added a fifty to the pile on the counter. "This taps us out."

The guard looked satisfied. "It was a big empty van. Put her stuff way in the back. They said they had several more loads to get on before they got to L.A."

Abe and Adele looked at each other resignedly. They nodded to the guard and returned to the crisp night air.

"What do you think?" Adele asked.

Abe studied the star-studded sky that usually accompanied the drop in temperature in Pauliapolis. "Have you had dinner? I'm starving."

Chapter

15

Surprising himself, Abe managed not to express his frustration until he had ordered his dinner. "Damn it. Until now, there was just a hunch that there might be a story, and maybe not much of one at that. Now we know that there is a story, a big one, but we'll probably never get near it."

"What do you think prompted the woman to move? Fear? Or a better offer than twenty-five thousand?" Adele mused as she buttered one part of the roll she had halved and quartered.

"With as little as we know, it could be either one," Abe said as he shook his head. "The first thing to speculate about is who got to her to scare her or buy her silence?"

Adele shook her head to suggest that the question was no mystery. "There's a very short list of people who knew that there was a story being offered. Only Henry Burton and the Sentinel's owner besides you and me."

"Why would Henry authorize me to pay for a story if the paper had decided to kill it? He could just have told us that the paper had decided not to buy and that would have been the end of it for us."

Adele was the picture of disbelief. "You're being naive. Henry, not to mention the owner, looks clean by telling you to proceed even though other arrangements had already been made. An editor's the owner's boy, even more than we are. That's always the case. Henry's a better man than most newspaper management, but he's not a paragon."

Abe shook his head in disagreement. "He never asked me for the phone number. He couldn't even have told me how to contact the woman, let alone do it himself."

Adele shrugged, "So he is just a link in the chain, but he's part of it."

"Maybe not," Abe persisted. "He might have known no more about what was going to happen than we did. Suppose he told Etheridge and the publisher told him to proceed with an offer. Then Etheridge gets in touch with his buddy the senator to spike the story in the several hours before my phone call was scheduled."

"Abe Fuller," Adele smiled, her expression revealing a touch of admiration, "you are quaint in your support of your boss the editor. However, that's not a bad scenario for what could have happened. Regardless which of us has the correct scenario, his telling us to proceed covers their tracks."

"What do you have against Burton?" Abe asked.

"Nothing," Adele protested with a wave of her hand. "I told you; he's better than the general run of them, but it's best to have no illusions. An editor's an editor."

"It sounds like one of them has soured you on anyone who holds the title," said Abe. "Care to tell me about it?"

Adele spotted the waiter approaching with their dinners. "It's not a story that goes well with food," she said and turned her attention to the steak that was being set before her.

Eating kept the hungry diners silent for a few minutes. Abe broke the silence with the comment that it was perhaps too late this evening to inform Henry Burton about the outcome of their efforts to purchase the story from the woman they now knew as Penelope Dayton.

"Right," Adele said wryly and rolled her eyes. "Besides, the surprise might overwhelm him."

"Wouldn't you be the one that's surprised if he told us to follow up and try to get the story anyway?" Abe said before raising a fork holding a cut of meat to his mouth.

"No, I wouldn't be surprised. That would play out the little cover story, wouldn't it?" Adele responded with a pedagogical air.

"Even if your cynical analysis is right, which I doubt, we'd still have the chance to go after the story," Abe reasoned.

"Until we got tired of wasting our time," said Adele.

"Maybe you just can't think of anyplace to start," challenged Abe.

"Don't be ridiculous," Adele grumbled once she had swallowed a mouthful and again assumed her instructional air. "First you've got to find the woman."

"Easily enough said. How?" asked Abe as though he were an insightful student challenging a teacher.

"The moving company has her address, obviously," Adele stated contemptuously.

"And why should they give it to you?"

Adele began to answer but stopped before the first word escaped.

"I can think of a way. But what's the point? She isn't going to tell us anything now that she's been bought off."

"That's what we deal with after we find her," Abe said optimistically.

"You're not telling me how you'd get the address because you don't want to work together on this, right?"

"Don't be ridiculous. I just don't want to waste time on a story that the paper won't print even if we get it," Adele leveled.

"It would be fun anyhow," Abe offered. "Come on, tell me what you'd do."

Adele pushed aside her now empty plate and looked at Abe with a grin. "I'd call the moving company and tell them that I have finished cleaning the very expensive oriental rug that the lady had left with us two weeks ago. Obviously she's forgotten in her haste to give us a forwarding address and we want to know where to ship it."

Abe put down his utensils and thought briefly. "We'd have to pick an actual company to pretend we're from. What if the movers check with the apartment building management?"

"Then we're dead, but why would they check?"

Abe was pleased. "We do it tomorrow morning whether Henry says to stay on the story or not, O.K.?"

"If you want," Adele answered as she looked about for the waiter with the look of someone overdue for her coffee. "But I'm not going to spend a lot of time on this. We either get a solid lead or we give it up," she added emphatically.

Abe nodded agreement. He then realized that he and Adele had both been using plural pronouns in their most recent exchanges. Though he was pleased at the development himself, he thought it best that he did not call attention to the fact for fear of loosing a barrage of defensive sarcasm from his attractive colleague.

When they had both had a couple sips of their coffee, Abe decided to hazard a personal inquiry. "Now that the food's been disposed of, are you ready to tell me the reason for your suspicious attitude toward editors as a species?"

Adele's eyes left Abe and surveyed the entire room, never really returning to look directly at Abe. "Forget what I said. I spoke without thinking. Henry Burton is a good boss."

"I can see that you get your stories by being honest with your sources. If you lied, even to a blind man, your voice would give you away," Abe said wryly.

"I wish what you say were true," Adele sighed penitently. "I've done my share of fudging to get the whole story from my sources many times. I'm embarrassed to think of how often."

"I'm sure it was always for a worthy reason," Abe offered. He surprised himself at his earnestness in rejecting Adele's self-criticism.

Adele raised her eyebrows in surprise. "What's this? A new you who's going to cut me some slack?"

"Come on," Abe chided, "I never beat on you except to have a little fun."

"And I've returned the barbs in the same spirit."

"So let's be straight with each other for a minute," Abe coaxed. "What's this attitude about editors? You got to admit it's a major matter if it slips out at unguarded moments."

"Wow," Adele smiled, "both a journalist and a psychiatrist. Those are rare in our business."

"Actually," Abe responded disingenuously, "I'm more of a psychic.

I think that you had a bad experience with an editor." Abe rubbed his forehead as though lost in thought, "Wait, wait, it's coming to me, Friedman. Yes, that's it. You had a bad experience with an editor named Friedman."

"Brilliant," Adele mumbled, caught between amusement and disgust.

"So you married the boss?" Abe said quietly, having no desire to draw her anger with his farfetched inference.

"No," Adele said focusing on her coffee cup with a wistful expression. "I was married to a reporter who became an editor."

"And he changed drastically when he became the boss," Abe inferred.

"He did not, oh great psychic," Adele said with mild sarcasm. "I gave up a good job to move to where his editor's job was. But when I got the job here, which pays as much as we were making together on that small town daily, he wouldn't come with me because it meant being a reporter again. The commuting marriage didn't work," she said and lapsed into silence. Abe nodded and studied Adele with a previously unused expression of sympathy.

Adele looked Abe in the eye and said, "Now we're going to drop this subject." She took another sip of coffee and looked at Abe with a wan smile. "Why don't you make a contribution to this therapy session? Why aren't you married?"

"What makes you think I'm not?"

"Please," Adele scoffed. "You spend so much time at the paper or out on the job that a wife would have filed a missing person report long ago."

Abe said tersely, "I got dumped."

"You're divorced?"

Abe nodded reflectively. "I never got far enough for that. She dumped me a couple weeks before the wedding."

Adele frowned. "That's a serious case of cold feet. Or was there something more concrete?"

Abe paused. He was reluctant to reveal something he had never shared with anyone, even when the hurt was fresh and unburdening himself might have helped. Revealing an old wound was even harder. He looked at Adele closely. He saw no look on her face that warned of her responding with barbed banter. He was surprised to find himself thinking that she was as near to a friend as he had in his life at the moment. He wondered whether that was a recognition of the pathetic quality of his life or the comfort and security he felt with this woman.

Abe sighed and looked away before he began. "I was under attack by some religious conservatives for a piece I'd written. She wanted me to apologize for what I'd written to calm down her father, who was never one of my biggest fans. Finally it came to an ultimatum that I apologize or the wedding was off. I couldn't apologize."

"Well, Mr. Abe Fuller," Adele said looking at him earnestly, "you should congratulate yourself on a narrow escape."

"You really think so?"

"Unless you like traveling a series of roads filled with pain that have an inescapable dead end."

"Yeh, you're probably right. Anyway, it was a long time ago."

A lengthy silence followed during which Abe felt surprisingly comfortable.

"So we'll meet with Henry first thing in the morning," Abe said as he reached for his coat.

Adele got up to begin her own departure. "But we're going to nose around a bit whether he says to look into the story or not, right?"

"Sure; absolutely," Abe said. He showed not sign of his pleasure at the chance to work together with Adele.

Buttoning her coat against the night time cold, Adele took her car keys from her pocket and asked, "Can I give you a lift?"

Abe shook his head. "Thanks, but I have to make a stop before I go home. I'll get a cab later." The truth was, he had no errand to do. He wanted to walk and think, but it was not any story for the paper that he had on his mind. Nor did he intend to dwell on the past; it was the future that had captured his attention. He wanted to think about what might develop from this cooperative venture, and not just the journalistic side of it.

Chapter

16

Abe and Adele agreed that Henry Burton was either a wonderfully skilled actor or he was genuinely surprised to learn of the unexpected development in the attempt to buy a supposedly sensational political story offered by the blonde mystery woman. There was a brief session of commiseration, sincerely expressed on Burton's part, and responded to with a gloomy, though feigned, expression of defeat by his two reporters. Adele and Abe exited the editor's office laboring at looking disappointed.

Anxious to pursue the story, they hastened to Adele's office to begin their effort. Adele sat behind her desk and reached for the yellow pages. Thumbing through the thick volume, Adele said, "I figure that if I stick to the big moving outfits, in about a half-dozen calls I should hit on the company that moved Penelope Dayton's stuff."

Abe sat in the chair that faced the desk and suggested blandly, "Call Midwest Movers."

"What's that? A hunch?" Adele asked.

"No," Abe answered with a look of self-satisfaction that he made no attempt to conceal. "I stopped back at Penelope's apartment building last night and pried it out of the security guard with a fifty dollar bill."

"Nice work, Abe," Adele smiled approvingly. Abe was certain that two days ago Adele's approval would have come in the form of a backhanded remark. He could not decide whether it was this new mode of Adele's approval or the former one that he would prefer as their regular style of dialogue, but the change was pleasant for variety's sake.

Adele waited impatiently for a response to the call she had initiated. "Hello, is this Midwest Movers?" she said after a brief pause. Shortly she began a representation she had obviously rehearsed. "This is the Rug Doctors, the carpet cleaners. We understand that you are moving the household things of a Ms. Penelope Dayton from the Riverside Towers, correct? You have already? But we have the oriental rug she left for cleaning. It's wrapped and ready for delivery. She never mentioned it? You're kidding? A ten thousand dollar rug and she never mentioned it? So now what do we do with it? Of course it's not your problem. Tell you what. Give us her new address and we will ask her if she'll pay to have it shipped. The Fairmount Apartments, University Drive, Beverly Hills, California, 90215. Got it. Thank you."

Adele triumphantly held up the notepad on which she had written the address. Abe gently clapped his hands together and looked at Adele admiringly.

"Did your j school professors teach you such deviousness or is it natural talent?"

"A little of both, I must confess," Adele grinned.

Abe rubbed his chin thoughtfully. "So we have an address on the west coast. What should we do with it?"

"Go see her, obviously," Adele proposed.

"We can't both go," Abe reasoned. "If we both took time off, Henry would get suspicious and want an explanation."

"One of us has to take some vacation time to visit a sick relative," Adele suggested.

"Yeh, I guess that would work," Abe agreed. "Of course, she probably isn't there yet, if she's driving her car out rather than having it shipped.

"Just as well," Adele said. "I'll need some time to get ready and set up some coverage of my work."

"Hold on," Abe protested, "how did this suddenly become your story?"

"It's not my story, Abe," Adele countered. "I just think that she's less likely to be scared off by a woman at this point. Whether she's been bought off or scared off, it will take some convincing to get her to tell us what she knows."

"And you think that you can be more convincing?" Abe huffed.

"Will you pull in your competitive horns," Adele chided. "I just think she'll find a woman less threatening. And I'm not going to steal the story from you. I promise."

After a moment's pause, Abe nodded. "You're probably right. O.K., you go. Let me know if there's anything you want me to do to cover for you."

"Thank you," Adele said. "And remember, I can't guarantee that I'll come back with anything."

"Understood," Abe said as he started for the door. "But good luck," he added with a genuine smile.

"I'll need it," Adele said to his back.

Chapter

17

A week after Adele and Abe agreed that she should be the one to try to meet with Penelope Dayton at her new location on the west coast, Adele was riding in a cab on University Avenue in Beverly hills. She studied the well-manicured grounds in the neighborhood consisting of a mixture of large single-family dwellings and apartment buildings that seemed to have been limited in scale so as not to overwhelm the single residences. The private homes were so beautifully kept that Adele hoped that they would escape the eventual pattern of large residences being sub-divided into apartments or business offices when a neighborhood began its a decline into urban blight.

The apartment buildings looked as though they catered to occupants whose affluence matched that of what was necessary to maintain a single family residence in the area. Apparently, Penelope Dayton's clientele was select enough and forthcoming enough to support her living in circumstances that offered both beauty and discretion. In some instances, Adele mused, the maxim about the wages of sin needed revising.

At the Fairmount apartments, Adele winced inwardly when she paid the substantial cab fare from the airport. As with the price of her plane ticket, she would not be claiming a reimbursement from the

Sentinel unless her unassigned investigation turned into a story that the paper would use. She approached the formidable looking man behind the lobby security desk with as confident an air as she could muster.

"Hello," she smiled at the hard face atop the uniformed set of broad shoulders, "I'm here to see Ms. Dayton."

"She expecting you?"

"No," Adele answered more calmly than she felt, "but if you tell her Adele Friedman from Pauliapolis is here to see her, she'll want to see me." While the guard picked up his phone and called Dayton's apartment, Adele wondered what her next move should be if Dayton refused to see her.

After the security guard identified Adele as the visitor and listened briefly, he looked to Adele and said, "She doesn't want to see you."

Adele gestured with her hand to keep the guard from cutting off the call and said, "Tell her that I have a message from the senator."

The guard relayed the statement into the phone and listened again. He said into the phone, "Yes, she's alone." After listening briefly again, he looked up at Adele and said, "You can go up. Eighth floor, apartment B, elevators over there," he concluded and pointed toward the end of the lobby.

Adele quickly made her way to the elevator and used the short ride up to consider what she could say immediately to Penelope Dayton so that the meeting would not end shortly after it began. On the eighth floor, Adele had only a few moments to wait after pressing the bell of apartment B before the door opened. Adele had before her a beautiful blonde who was surely the woman that Abe had described, perhaps, surprisingly, in understatement. Adele spoke quickly, "Ms. Dayton, I lied about having a message from Senator Brockhurst, I'm really here to tell you the Sentinel will pay the twenty-five thousand you requested for your story."

Penelope Dayton registered impatience and disgust. "You think if I were interested in that deal any longer that I've have moved rather than wait for Abe Fuller's call?" With that question, she began to close the door.

Adele took a step forward and put her hand out to keep the door from closing. "Maybe we'll up the price. Please just tell me what you want."

Dayton moved forward to look up and down the hall. Adele had observed that there seemed to be only two apartments per floor; hence it was not surprising that there was no traffic in the hall. Through clenched lips, Penelope Dayton said, "What I want is for you to go away and never, never bother me again."

"Maybe if you give me five minutes off the record I can increase the chances that neither I nor no one else will ever bother you about your experiences in Pauliapolis," Adele proposed. She didn't know for certain what she meant herself by the assertion, but she realized it was paramount to simply keep the conversation going.

"Lady," Dayton began dryly, "that's supposed to have been covered in my deal."

Adele gave a palms up gesture suggesting Dayton's point had been made. "My being here demonstrates that your arrangements, whatever they are, could be improved. You ought to have some insurance. I can tell you how to get it."

Penelope studied Adele appraisingly for s time. "Come on in," she nodded and added emphatically, "for a few minutes."

Adele entered and smiled in admiration at the luxuriousness and tastefulness of the spacious living room in which she found herself. She had not seen Dayton's quarters in Pauliapolis but could not imagine them to have been more pleasant than these surroundings. Obviously, Dayton had not fled in panic and seized the first haven she could find just to get out of town. Adele suppressed the urge to tell Dayton that she could see that there was a lot of overhead in her line of work. Deciding that she would not be invited to sit, Adele took the liberty of seating herself on the nearest of two ivory-colored couches covered in a finely textured silk fabric. She noted the love-seat size of the couches and suppressed the temptation to ask if the choice of size had been deliberate.

As Dayton sat on the facing couch, Adele said, "Abe Fuller and I were mystified at your sudden loss of interest in money. As I said before, the paper authorized us to pay what you asked for the political story that you offered for sale."

"I have not lost interest in money, Ms. Friedman. I was paid much,

much more than I asked of the paper not to sell the story at all. I've never really understood the old saw about silence being golden till now."

"If silence paid so well, why did you leave town?" Adele asked.

"Relocation to the city of my choice at no cost to myself was a part of the deal." Dayton made a sweeping gesture of her arms toward her surroundings. "Not bad, don't you think?"

Adele smiled. "I could probably bear it myself." She met Dayton eye-to-eye. "You sure these generous people can be trusted?"

"Everything promised has been delivered," Dayton said with satisfaction.

"Do you feel safe?" Adele asked.

"I am safe, as long as I keep my mouth shut."

"Or until the story breaks in a way that connects you with it," Adele said as placidly as she could, "even if you haven't said anything."

"You don't have a story to break, and you're sure as hell not going to get one from me," Dayton said emphatically.

"I'm not talking about my having anything to write now--or even later." Adele shook her head knowingly. "Political scandals, unlike secrets on other topics, have a way of surfacing sooner or later."

Dayton smiled with a confidence equal to Adele's. "I'd agree with you if I hadn't had a few big time politicians who were among the secrets on my client list in North Louisiana. No doubt I will have them and others among my clients here in California."

Adele returned the smile. "You're forgetting to distinguish how political sex stories differ other sex stories. Or maybe you do. Some sex stories can be open secrets of no notoriety for years. You described the story you wanted to sell as a political story. My guess is that it's not so much about the sex but about cheating or money, or that all time journalistic favorite, the cheating about money parlay."

Dayton's silence and expressionless told Adele that she might not be on target but she was not wildly off base either. "Have you considered that you'd be safest if the story got out in a version that didn't name you as a source, even if you were a participant."

"What do you mean?"

"A story for which someone else is named as the source puts you in the clear in a definitive way, but a secret that gets out anonymously is one where the injured parties could accuse you as the source whether you leaked it or not."

"Don't tell me that you've ever gotten a story out of someone with that convoluted crap," Dayton snorted derisively.

"You would be surprised," Adele smiled.

"Yes, I would."

"The process I speak of is simple," Adele said. "Instead of someone giving the reporter the whole story or even any incriminating piece of it to which the source could be tied, someone provides a vague hint that can be followed up. Since the story is developed from the reporter's investigation, if it can be developed at all, it would truthfully have been built from sources other than that vague hint. The story's out and the person whose safety has been tied to keeping the story hidden is in better shape than when there was a secret that the person might be blamed for letting out."

Dayton's crooked smile was an indication of her skepticism.

Adele said, "I would think that someone so successful in your line of work is exceptionally skilled at vagueness."

"And even more skilled at guarding her own best interests," Dayton retorted. Adele could think of no additional argument to make. She sat quietly looking at her beautiful host. Finally, Penelope Dayton stood and walked toward the door, obviously an indication that she wanted Adele to leave.

Adele rose and reluctantly started toward the door. After she had passed the threshold, Dayton, who had been holding the door open, said, "It's great news about the new pro football team in Pauliapolis." From the hall, Adele turned back to face Dayton, but the other woman had already closed the door.

Chapter

18

be Fuller's brow wrinkled with puzzlement and frustration. "That's it? All she said was that it's great about the pro football team?" Abe shook his head from side-to-side in dismay.

"I was lucky to get that much out of her," Adele repeated wearily. "Why should she say anything at all? She's been very well paid and re-located to what I assure you is a very pleasant location. No doubt she's been cautioned about what would happen to her if she lets the story, whatever it is, out."

"Well, if we do turn up anything," Abe snorted, "whoever it's about sure as hell couldn't say we got it from her."

"Whatever the story is, it's got something to do with Senator Brockhurst. We know that much," Adele said with conviction.

"And we know that why?" Abe asked skeptically.

"Her initial approach was that she had a political story to tell. Second, she let me up to her apartment because I said I had a message from Brockhurst."

"Yeh," Abe countered, "but if we take her seriously about the Loggers football team being her hint, then there is supposed to be a connection between Brockhurst and the team, and there isn't any."

Adele responded quickly. "True, there's no direct connection such as owning stock or the like, but he put a lot of work into helping the group from the city to get the franchise, didn't he?"

"Yeh, but so did every major politician in the state: the mayor, the governor, every legislator who saw that supporting it as worth some votes in the next election," Abe reasoned.

"You're sure Brockhurst isn't one of the investors?" Adele asked as she doodled aimlessly on the pad on her desk.

"Not absolutely," Abe admitted. "But he's not listed in any of the obligatory paperwork. His involvement isn't even likely in some indirect fashion. He'd have been committing political suicide to have backed the franchise application effort so strongly and supported the stadium project as he did if he'd had a personal involvement."

Adele rested her head on her hand and showed the fatigue of her recent travel and the effort to catch up on her duties after her return.

"Maybe Penelope Dayton wasn't trying to give me a hint at all. Maybe she's just a football fan.

Abe looked again at the walls of Adele's office, as though he expected the appearance of a message on the wall that obviously wasn't there yet. "Maybe we should approach the subject from a different angle. What person would have most likely been Dayton's source for the political story that she was going to sell until it was more lucrative not to sell it? My guess would be a client. Let's think about who Dayton's customer might have been who spilled the relevant information."

Adele hunched her shoulders reflecting her indecision. "Do you suppose her client and the ownership of the Loggers are linked somehow?"

"A juicy story about one of the owners and a hooker would be a long way from anything anyone would call a sensational political story," Abe judged and added, "Maybe her mention of the Loggers was intended to lead us away from the trail leading to a political story into a dead end."

Adele mused, "Sex, politics and sports, not an unheard mixture. I think it needs to be checked out," she asserted. "Why don't I look into the possibility that the Loggers ownership could be involved in a questionable political matter? Meanwhile you could try to find out if Penelope Dayton had any clients with heavy weight political connections."

"I can do that," Abe nodded. "Since the lady's left town, the security guys at her former apartment building or the doorman wouldn't fear repercussions for identifying pictures of her frequent visitors--for a fee, of course. However, I can't figure how you're going to dig into the possibility of improper political involvement by Loggers' ownership?"

"You forget that we may have a person in the league commissioner's office who would love to get the league office in front of a looming scandal," Adele grinned. Abe looked puzzled. Adele prompted, "Remember my column last week, under your name, of course, about Mike Mercutio of the pro league commissioner's staff? He might be receptive to answering a few questions from a reporter from the same paper that gave him such a favorable write up. I'll call him and be my most ingratiating self. I think he'd level with me if any ethical or political wrinkles had to be ironed out before the Logger owners were awarded the franchise."

"You're expecting a lot from a phone call to a source you've only talked to once to get info for someone else's puff piece," Abe offered discouragingly.

"If he is reluctant to talk on the phone, I'll offer to go see him," Adele said with more eagerness than Abe expected to hear.

Abe raised his eyebrows. "I suppose Mike's stayed in pretty good shape since he retired as a player."

"Your point being?" Adele asked.

"It crossed my mind that you might have another reason than pursuing the story for getting together with Mike Mercutio," Abe offered as a playful accusation.

"It hadn't crossed my mind," Adele asserted, "but I'll consider it."

"Let's keep it professional, Friedman," Abe said, not sure in his own mind why he had brought the subject up. Since the Dayton story had developed, he and Adele had blunted the sharpness of the relentless banter which had been their usual mode of dialogue until recently. It seemed inappropriate to resort to that style of interaction now.

Adele smiled coyly, "You doubt my being able to keep separate the social and the professional?"

"O.K., I've got things to do," Abe said, choosing to extricate himself from a situation that he had suddenly become uneasy with by avoiding her question. While Abe was leaving, Adele still carried her inscrutable smile.

Adele set about her task immediately. She shared Abe's doubts that Mercutio would discuss on the phone a sensitive matter such as an owner's unethical conduct. However, because the pro football league commissioner's office was thousands of miles from Pauliapolis, North Louisiana, to go there would require several days absence from the Sentinel. She did not see how she could plausibly make an excuse to leave town so soon after her trip to Los Angeles less than a week earlier. Yet although the subject she intended to raise with Mike Mercutio might be deemed too sensitive to discuss by phone, Adele concluded that an attempt to get information by phone had to be made.

When she gave her name to Mercutio's secretary and identified herself as a reporter from the Pauliapolis Sentinel, the woman's reluctance to connect her to Mercutio bordered on rudeness. However, when Mercutio took her call his voice sounded quite amiable. "This is Mike Mercutio, Ms. Friedman," Mercutio said. "What can I do for you?"

"I'm looking into doing a story on the award of the expansion franchise to the group from Pauliapolis, and I'd like to ask you some questions," Adele said.

"The decision on the franchise was pretty much settled before I joined the commissioner's office," Mercutio said. "I'll need a little time to round up some information before I can be very responsive to your questions."

"Should I call back in a day or so?" Adele said suspecting that she was being put off until some evasive non-answers could be developed.

"Actually, I have a better idea. I have to be in Pauliapolis next week. Some details about the new franchise's special opportunity to draft players are being finalized. Why don't we have lunch and I'll be ready to answer all your questions?"

"I didn't know that part of your duties with the commissioner's office is cultivating the media," Adele said.

"It's not; I have wanted to see you again since the interview you did with me," Mercutio responded and added, "You know, one retired jock to another."

"Really?" Adele murmured, with surprise at Mike's choice of words.

"Oh, come on," Mercutio asserted. "You're not going to go all humble on me and be surprised I know about your basketball career?"

"I assure you excessive humility has never been one of my problems. I'm flattered, actually."

"Then we're on for lunch," Mercutio said with satisfaction.

"Yes, of course."

"I'll give you a call on time and place after I get town. I'm looking forward to it, Ms. Friedman."

"Adele," she offered.

"Right, Adele. See your then, Adele," Mercutio said preparing to break off.

"Mike," Adele injected, hurrying to keep Mercutio on the line. "I don't want to blind side you with my questions when we have lunch. I'm looking into the possibility of Senator Brockhurst's involvement with the Loggers' ownership group."

"O.K." Mercutio responded easily. "I'll find out everything there is to know about the who and how of the process. You know that the league tries to keep these things as open as possible. I'll be ready for your questions. However, I certainly don't want all our time spent on business."

"It would be nice to avoid that," Adele said, surprising herself that a bit of throatiness had entered her voice.

"I'm looking forward to it, Adele," Mercutio emphasized as their conversation ended.

Adele sat pondering the arrangement she had made. Mike Mercutio's interest in socializing with her was obvious. She had not been involved with anyone since the break up of her marriage. In fact, she had not so much as had what could properly be called a date. In truth, she couldn't even say she had missed a man's being interested in her. Of course, there was a professional reason behind this lunch. Adele wondered if a problem could develop out her having agreed to lunch rather than a simple interview. She did not want a bruised male ego preventing her having what help, if any, Mercutio might give with the story she was pursuing. She would have to do her best to make lunch predominantly business with only a modicum of pleasantry.

Later, Abe Fuller looked up from behind his desk at Adele and squinted as he said again, "Lunch?" as although the word denoted some toxic chemical.

"Oh, you do grasp the concept," Adele responded with the expression of a teacher whose student had just understood the principle of relativity.

"You couldn't have pushed him very hard or you might have gotten something out of the phone call besides the chance to chat over lunch," Abe accused. "Is this guy a potential source or does your interest lie in some other area of activity?"

"How could I possibly be interested in a single, handsome, successful lawyer and executive when I'm around a charmer like you, Fuller?" Adele retorted with some embarrassment.

"So you're not charmed by me. Excuse me while I head for the river to drown myself. I just want to be sure you remember that we going after a story here," Abe countered defensively.

"Don't you worry about me holding up my end. You just see that you come up with something yourself," Adele said and turned away from Abe's cubicle.

Before she managed more than a couple steps Abe said, "I already have." Adele turned and showed her skepticism. "While you were busy working on your social calendar, I went over to the Riverside Towers with fistful of pictures and asked the security guard if any of the men was a frequent visitor of Penelope Dayton. He picked out Harold Fortner. He said that Fortner was there often enough and long enough lately that he ought to have shared the rent. No doubt he chipped in a lot more than part of the rent."

Adele sat down in the chair beside Abe's desk. "So whatever story the lady had to sell, it probably came from Fortner."

"Yeh, but at the moment we have no idea what it might have been," mused Abe.

"Oh, come on, Fuller," Adele scoffed. "Sensational political stories are either about sex or money. Fortner's personal life wouldn't be a big time story even if he's having hourly sex with a high end professional playmate. The story must be about money."

"You have a very cynical view of human nature, Friedman--cynical but accurate," Abe grinned. "So where do we go from here?"

"Here's an idea," Adele said with exaggerated brightness to emphasize that she thought the next steps were obvious. "I'll do lunch and you look at Fortner's activities to see if there's anything dubious that he's doing on Brockhurst's behalf."

"Not a promising possibility," Abe rejected. "There isn't even a Brockhurst presidential campaign yet."

"You know as well as I do that the whole concept of the campaign consultant is dubious," Adele said. "It introduces the worst aspects of commercial marketing to the political process."

"However, consultants have become so routine that nothing they're involved in would shock the public," Abe retorted.

Adele stood and began her exit. "That being true until now has not kept campaign consultants from becoming an increasingly significant factor in contemporary politics. Maybe Fortner will be the first one to reach a level of scumminess to cause more than a ripple of public outrage."

Abe applauded Adele's exiting form, not quite sure whether it was her last remark or the woman herself to which he was showing approval.

Chapter

19

What Abe wanted to find out was: in the moments of respite from Fortner's amorous activities with Penelope Dayton (assuming such moments had occurred), what scandalous information might Harold Fortner have revealed about the nascent political campaign of Senator Randall Brockhurst for his party's presidential nomination? To answer the question was well nigh impossible, since there was no witness to the pillow talk. All he could do was reason about circumstances and decide if an avenue of exploration--a next step toward an answer--presented itself.

Randall Brockhurst had exhibited statesmanlike qualities during his three plus terms in the senate. He could be bipartisan without surrendering his principles; he exhibited consistent concern for the public interest; he would disagree with his own party leadership if common sense demanded it; yet he had always been respected as a sound party man. In short, he carried no negative baggage that would eliminate him as a contender for his party's nomination. If he ran, Brockhurst was a cinch for a favorite son nomination from the state's delegation.

However, what he lacked was the large-scale political base that comes from representing a large population. Though North Louisiana was huge in land area, it had scant population. That fact was reflected in the size of the state's delegation to the nominating convention. Even if he had the support of the entire North Louisiana delegation to the nominating convention, he was nowhere near the support that a favorite son candidate from one of the populous states would have.

The scant number of the senator's initial delegate count was not in itself sufficient to squelch Brockhurst's chances. Consequently, he would have to build support in the state primaries before the nominating convention. Money, that essential grease of the American political process, was the ingredient needed for a favorite son candidate to survive beyond the early stages of the long primary campaign. That essential ingredient was more readily available to aspirants from urbanized, populous states. Aspirants from states with large commercial and industrial enterprises not only have money more readily available, but have it in astronomical amounts compared with the resources of a candidate from a state that is not only sparse in population but also in the number of corporations doing business or headquartered within it.

Harold Fortner, a heavyweight political consultant, was much in demand in this year where there is no incumbent president running for re-election and no dominating frontrunner in either party. He knew the realities of delegate mathematics and money better than anyone. Why was he here in North Louisiana, working for one of those long shot possibilities that regularly fell by the wayside early in the excruciatingly long presidential primary process for lack of dollars and delegates? Of course he could, and probably would, be hired by one of the survivors in the latter stages of the winnowing process if Brockhurst dropped out. Yet his intimate knowledge of the political process could have led him to one of the more likely contenders to begin with. Why was Fortner here with a political aspirant about whom the final assessment would likely be, "a good man with much to offer, but--" Why not ask him why he's here, perhaps a bit obliquely, but ask him, Abe concluded

When Abe made the request for an interview with Fortner, he said it was to ask the respected political campaign consultant about the particular circumstances facing a presidential hopeful from a state with a small delegate and financial base. The topic was sufficiently broad and non-threatening enough that Senator Brockhurst saw no problem that the interviewee be Fortner rather than himself. As to Fortner, he expressed eagerness to do the interview both as an opportunity to aid his employer and to talk about the dynamics of the electoral process that was his passion.

Fortner bordered on the effusive as he invited Abe to sit on the leather couch in his office as the political operative seated himself in a chair placed at a right angle to the couch. "My understanding is that you're a sportswriter," Fortner stated, his face registering an amiable curiosity.

"Primarily," Abe said as he settled in and flipped open a notepad.

"What brings you to do an obvious political interview?" Fortner asked.

Abe took a moment to assess the physical being opposite before he answered. Fortner was a tall man whose body tended to bulkiness. His face, however, was angular rather than soft, as one might have expected from a middle-aged body beginning to acquire padding. His demeanor radiated confidence and a suggestion that it would be unwise to under-estimate him.

"You might not have noticed that the baseball season is ending rather ingloriously for the Stags and winter sports are not yet underway. Consequently, covering baseball gets to the level of writing a daily obituary at the end of the kind of season the team's had. The size of the Sentinel staff is limited enough that one is tempted to look for feature ideas beyond one's usual area of writing. Occasionally one hits on an idea that looks promising enough that pitching it to the managing editor gets one a nod to write it. Of course, sometimes the idea is promising enough that the editor assigns it to the reporter whose primary assignment is to that area. If that colleague likes the work done to that point and doesn't mind teaming up, we often end up working on the idea together. Obviously, the possibility that the state may have a presidential contender is a high interest political topic."

"So is this is a topic on which you might eventually be working with your charming colleague Ms. Friedman?" Fortner inferred.

Abe smiled that Fortner had not failed to notice in a single meeting the attractiveness of Adele, something which he himself had taken a couple years to become aware of. "You have a very good memory of her after nothing more than a brief meeting. Of course, Mrs. Friedman is well-known on the paper for her exacting journalistic standards. I will need to draft something rather meaningful about the way a big time campaign effort like the senator's would be designed and executed before she will agree to work with me."

"Let's not get ahead of ourselves," Fortner cautioned. "The senator hasn't announced, and may not unless we find that there's some realistic chance to make a successful run."

Abe hastened his assurance. "Oh, I understand that. In fact, that's the tack I was thinking of taking for my piece. To take a look at the special difficulties faced by an aspirant from a sparsely populated state, no matter how well-qualified he is."

"I'm glad you recognize that the senator is a well-qualified candidate. From my point of view, it's a pleasure to have a client that's an easy sell. His voting record, his position on the issues and his personal attributes all should be favorably reacted to by his party's delegates and later the electorate at large," Harold Fortner said, going quickly into a campaigning mode.

"This seems like one of those times when the senator's party has at least a half dozen potential choices with similar profiles," Abe offered. "And several of them are from states with a lot more clout in the party than North Louisiana, unfortunately for the senator."

"That's true, but that similarity of profiles assures Senator Brockhurst's competitiveness in the early stages of the process. Within the group that is likely to draw early interest, he is as attractive as any of the others," Fortner rebutted.

"But he is realistically a long shot in the two categories of the number of favorite son delegates and financial support," Abe persisted. "He is apparently so much a long shot that he's even debating whether or not to announce."

"On the other hand, I'm here," Fortner asserted. The man seemed to puff up in his chair. His shoulders straightened and his chin lifted. The tilt of his head gave the effect of his looking down at Abe though they were the same height.

"I don't understand," Abe said, not certain what Fortner's terse statement implied.

"You think that I'd be here if there wasn't a serious possibility of the senator's not only announcing but being in the race until what promises to be a very open convention?" Fortner queried. The question conveyed as much about Fortner's sense of importance as it did about the candidacy of Senator Brockhurst.

"To be honest," Abe came back, "there is some mystery about your being here. You have been involved in a number of national campaigns and in one instance you were the campaign consultant of a president seeking re-election."

"No only seeking but succeeding," Fortner interjected.

"Which emphasizes my point," Abe continued. "That was the most prominent of a number of major involvements that you have had. So one wonders why you haven't hooked up with one of the big state aspirants. Among those are contenders from both parties. Since you've worked for candidates in both parties whose chances are more favorable than Senator Brockhurst's, I'd have expected you to have joined one of those aspirants already."

"Perhaps the senator's chances aren't as slim as you think," Fortner offered with a twisted grin which attempted mystery rather than amusement. "You, like many people, are focused on recent times, when each party's choice of candidate has been made before the convention. That has not always been the case. There have been many times when none of the aspirants came to the convention with enough delegates committed to be nominated on the first ballot. This is going to be one of those years. It gives an opportunity to those persons of character, accomplishment and attractive positions on the issues that voters care about to sell themselves to the convention. The prerequisite is that the aspirant has an effective campaign organization and fundraising effort that puts him into the open convention as a serious possibility."

Abe realized that, to this point, the dialogue had indicated nothing revealing or improper other than Fortner's ego, which could be given a number of unattractive labels but neither "scandalous" nor "illegal" would be among them. He tried to turn the subject. "How are you going to vitalize the senator's campaign? What are the steps in the process? What will it take for the senator to announce, and, if he does, what will be the next step to keeping his candidacy alive?"

Fortner adopted the mode of the master providing basic education

Anything You Can Do, I Can Do

to the totally uninitiated. Abe allowed for Fortner's having no way of knowing of his experience as a political journalist, but he felt that Fortner's approach might have been the same had Abe been a Nobel laureate in political science. Smiling as though he was revealing a great secret, Fortner began. "The senator is arguably the best qualified person among the likely contenders in his party. His voting record, his position on the significant issues and his personal background make him an easy sell. Since he is from a state which had little clout nationally, his strengths would not be significant if there were one or more aspirants who already had nationwide support, but there are none. Thus, the senator begins the race with some highly relevant advantages."

"But he hasn't announced yet," Abe pointed out. "What conditions have to be in place for him to take the plunge?"

Fortner continued pedantically. "To begin, he has to have the support of both the state party and the regional power structure. The party must elect a slate of delegates committed to supporting the senator unanimously as their favorite son candidate. The power structure must make its support tangible both vocally and financially."

"Those are major hurdles in themselves," Abe stated.

"I wouldn't be here if they were," Fortner said with evident self-assurance.

"Assuming you're correct about those initial hurdles having virtually been passed, how do you think the senator will fare in the primaries?" Abe asked.

"Not impressively at first. It will start out as a crowded field. As he becomes better known nationally, he will pick up support. Especially when the field begins to winnow as the long shots who run out of money drop out."

"Money won't be a problem for Brockhurst?" Abe asked with raised eyebrows. He knew that the number of inherited fortunes or corporations to make contributions in North Louisiana were not numerous.

Fortner looked at Abe with traces of disdain. "I never get involved in campaigns that are run on a shoe string."

"Do you actually think that Brockhurst can get enough delegates in the primaries to be a strong contender at the convention?" Abe asked skeptically.

Fortner straightened his shoulders and lifted his chin. He seemed to peer downward to look at Abe although they were of similar height and seated on the same level. It was the demeanor Fortner seemed to find appropriate to his being one of the anointed witch doctors of American elections.

"As I already said, no one will have the nomination locked up before the convention." Fortner pontificated.

"Really?" Abe queried, his wry grin showing doubt about Fortner's pronouncement.

"It's going to be an open convention," Fortner repeated in an oracular tone. The senator will get there with the unanimous support of the state delegation and some delegates won in the carefully chosen primaries where circumstances favor him. He'll do well in the big primaries near the end of the primary process. That base will stay solid through the early ballots at the convention. With those votes plus whatever he picks up in the early shifting of support, he will be in an excellent position to compete with the small group of contenders who remain after the early ballots."

Convinced that he was not going to steer Fortner into a misstep about the nascent campaign or an indiscrete personal revelation, Abe closed his notebook, "You are very convincing."

"Being convincing is my business," Fortner said confidently.

Abe had seen enough of Fortner to dislike him as a human being, but Fortner was too skilled a professional to say anything that would point toward the information that was so scandalous that Penelope Dayton thought it was worth twenty-five thousand dollars for her to repeat it for publication. He rose and pocketed the notebook that he had not had occasion to use much.

Abe smiled mechanically and extended his hand toward Fortner. "You have given me a good start on a piece about the circumstances of being a presidential aspirant from a sparsely populated state that has limited political clout."

Fortner gripped Abe's hand firmly. "Would you be willing to show me a draft of your piece before you submit it to your editor?"

"Sure," Abe agreed. "If I get something developed that I'm not ashamed to take to my colleague and my editor." As he left, Abe did feel a twinge of guilt. He should have told Fortner that the campaign consultant had a better chance of being elected president himself than of Abe ever showing him something he had written so that Fortner could paw over it before its publication.

Later, he reported to Adele the essence of his unrevealing dialogue with Fortner. She smiled in spite of her disappointment. "So all that not-so-unique insight into how the electoral process works didn't knock you out of your chair?"

Abe nodded forlornly. "Of course, being exposed to all that wisdom was inspiring."

Oh, well," Adele clasped her hands in feigned satisfaction, "at least it wasn't a total loss."

"Yeh," Abe said with matching cynicism, "now I can go back to covering the upcoming pro football season with renewed fervor." He stood and turned to leave, "I've got work to do."

"Well, hey, Abe," Adele offered consolingly, "it was worth a shot. Maybe something will turn up out of my lunch with Mike Mercutio next Tuesday."

Abe grumbled over his shoulder as he left. "Something might turn up, all right. But I doubt that will be about Brockhurst. Just try to keep it printable."

Adele looked after the retreating figure with openmouthed surprise. Either there was some history between Mike Mercutio and Abe that she didn't know about or Abe was feeling a twinge of jealousy. Adele smiled broadly and thought that she preferred that it be the latter.

Chapter

20

It was a crisp late fall day in Pauliapolis when Adele walked through the midday sunshine to meet Mike Mercutio from the pro football league commissioner's office for lunch. Her mood was uncertain. She knew Mercutio's interest in seeing her was purely social, which was not an unpleasant prospect. Yet her desire to explore the possibility of a compromising relationship between Randall Brockhurst and the ownership of the Loggers football team was uppermost in her mind. However, she did not want Mercutio to conclude that she accepted his invitation solely to pursue a story. She hoped to underscore that impression with the well-cut navy blue pants suit and the frilly pale blue blouse she was wearing under her tan suede coat. She had chosen the stylishly contoured suede coat rather than the all-weather khaki straight line outerwear which was her usual workday coat for this time of year. After all, this was the time of year when an early snow, a blustery rain or a clear cold sky were equally probable and the plain but practical all-weather coat was a sensible choice. Adele felt the occasion called for style over practicality.

In Mercutio's previous visit to Pauliapolis he must have schooled himself on the city center's better restaurants. He had chosen the only high quality Italian restaurant in the city, Don Giovanni's, which was in the best of the city's locally owned hotels. She crossed the hotel lobby toward the restaurant entry. Before she reached the host podium, she saw the man whose face was familiar not only from their one meeting but its occasional occurrences in the various media. Mike Mercutio rose from a leather chair near the restaurant entry. The dark gray suit hung well on what was still an athlete's body. Above the broad shoulders a square, strong face broke into a broad smile as he saw his partner for lunch approaching. He came toward her to offer his hand. "Adele," he said warmly as she extended her hand to grasp his hand.

"Hello, Mike," Adele responded. "I'm pleased to see you again."

"I got us a table with a view," Mercutio said and extended his arm to invite her to precede him across the room to a table next to the windows that offered a view of the river and its autumn-leaf splashed banks.

"I hope you're not on a tight schedule, Adele," Mercutio said as he reached to take the coat she had begun to remove. He draped it over one of the empty chairs and held out the one facing the view for Adele to be seated.

Adele wondered if his meticulous courtesy was a special effort or if he was behaving as he normally did. She studied him as he rounded the table to seat himself. At six feet, he was not tall as pro quarterbacks went, but ten years after retirement he maintained a trimness that few former pro players managed at his age. His close-cropped black hair curled defiantly but attractively.

After Adele had agreed to a glass of chardonnay while they considered the options for lunch, her host turned his deep brown eyes to her and said, "Before I get distracted into other matters, I want to ask you to pass along my thanks to your colleague Abe Fuller for that very flattering column that he wrote about me several weeks ago."

"I'm sure he'll appreciate hearing that you liked it." Adele responded with a broader than usual smile; she enjoyed the unusual situation of being asked to carry thanks to someone else for what she had written herself. "I know he got a lot of positive feedback on that piece. Yours is a very unusual story. Abe thinks that genuine football fans are fond of stories of players who rose to the occasion at a time of unusual challenge and opportunity, as you did." Adele wondered if Abe would approve of the words that she was putting in his mouth. Best not to ask him, she decided.

Mercutio blushed slightly at the praise. "I had a very brief moment in the limelight."

Adele found that endearing. Most of the jocks she knew seemed to feel that whatever accolades were heaped on them fell considerably short of what they deserved. "My dad is a football coach, as you know. You were his favorite kind of player. Someone who's as his best when crucially needed."

Mike smiled. "That makes him my favorite kind of coach."

Adele thought Mike Mercutio was growing more interesting by the minute. The waiter had returned with their wine and Adele took a sip as much to prevent her further complementing her host as for interest in the wine.

Mercutio had seated himself at right angles to Adele. He looked to his left at the blaze of color on the river banks and said, "Pauliapolis is a very pretty place. Do you enjoy living here?"

"You're seeing it at its best. The extremes in weather between mid-winter and mid-summer are a bit daunting," Adele said. "But I like the people, and I like my job."

"You grew up in this climate," Mike said. He must have familiarized himself with her background to know that her youth had been spent on the plains a few hundred miles to the west of Pauliapolis."

"I'm supposed to be the one that researches people's backgrounds," Adele smiled in response.

"Just curious about a fellow athlete," Mike explained, "And a very impressive one at that."

"I thought you said that you weren't in media relations," Adele queried with a little show of embarrassment.

"Sorry. I didn't mean to be intrusive," Mike smiled. "Why don't we order lunch?" he said and looked about for their waiter, who was solicitously near at hand.

Their chatting during lunch covered a variety of the sort personal subjects suitable to strangers becoming acquainted. When they were awaiting coffee, Adele realized that she had been just as guilty as Mike in keeping the conversation away from any subject that would have caused tension. She had quizzed him about what had attracted him to law school and why he had left private practice to join the commissioner's office. She had also responded at greater length than she had intended about her enjoyment of journalism and her feelings about its role in an open society. She had been downright preachy, but Mike did not seem to mind. In fact, he had seemed to enjoy her discourse.

However, it was past time to address the subject that had prompted her to call him in the first place. "I've really enjoyed myself, Mike, but I would like to get to my questions about the Loggers ownership, if you don't mind." She chided herself for the apologetic wording of her statement and struggled to put on her journalist's armament.

"Of course," Mike nodded agreeably. "I'm sorry that I've rambled on so. I've just enjoyed our talk. Let me cover some background that I think is probably familiar to you and perhaps that will give a context for your questions."

"That sounds helpful," Adele smiled in response to Mike's forthcoming opening. Rarely had she had an interview begun so cooperatively.

Mercutio donned a serious expression. "As I'm sure you know, the Loggers ownership group consists of six people. Sam Greywolf, who owns seventy-five percent of the team and five other men who hold five percent each of the stock."

"Yes," Adele nodded. "And it appears that Senator Brockhurst is not one of those five minority investors."

"It's more than appearance that he's not a stockholder, Adele. Each of those men is a successful entrepreneur in his own right. None of those men would be a party to being any kind of front man. They are all friends of Greywolf's. The word is that they are men who made a small investment because they enjoy the status of being connected to pro football. Greywolf formed an ownership group not because he needed help financially but because he wanted to accede to his friends' interest as football fans."

"They are also powerful men who like to have a political climate favorable to their interests," Adele pointed out. "In fact, there are a couple of them whose other business interests give them an incentive for a new stadium that goes beyond their wanting to enhance their investment in the team. The senator's help in getting the stadium agreement could be a motive for their rewarding him in some way other than stock, couldn't it?"

"Come on, Adele. Their stake in the team wouldn't make them ineligible to bid on the construction openly. Besides the campaign contribution laws limit what they could give to Senator Brockhurst directly." Mike's demeanor was not defensive. The lawyer in him was simply responding to the likely inferences that an earnest reporter might make.

"Yes, I guess," Adele frowned.

"What's this about, anyway?" Mike asked. "Is there something that has raised suspicion about the senator that has you looking into his circumstances."

Adele went eye-to-eye with Mike. "Nothing greatly suspicious. He's considering a run for the presidential nomination. For a long shot like him, money, particularly at the start of a campaign, is a more crucial factor than for the frontrunners with nationwide organizations. We're looking into the money angle." Adele was struck suddenly with pangs of regret about what she had said. "Mike, I hope you understand that I've spoke confidentially. I don't want to be the initiator of a damaging and false rumor about him within the leadership of professional football. The senator has a deservedly lofty reputation in this state."

"Understood," Mike responded reassuringly. "The league has as much interest as you do in not raising negative speculations. In fact, the commissioner's a bit paranoid about the possibility of a scandal involving the league. You're no doubt aware of the special arrangements that had to be made so that Sam Greywolf would qualify as a candidate for the franchise."

"I'm afraid I don't," Adele admitted. "I've just been here in Pauliapolis with the Sentinel about two years myself. I know the football franchise acquisition effort had been started well before that. What special circumstances had to be worked out for Greywolf?"

"Greywolf is an American Indian, which is obvious from his last name. The idea of having an owner of his ethnicity was very appealing to both the commissioner and a considerable majority of the current owners of the existing teams," Mike explained.

"So he was given preferential consideration?" Adele inferred.

"Not really," Mike nodded. "He was permitted to make a special arrangement to remove an obstacle that would have disqualified him from bidding for a franchise in a very competitive situation where half a dozen cities were bidding for the only new franchise to come up in over a decade."

"The man's got tons of money," Adele said. "The obstacle couldn't have been the funding a competitive bid."

"Far from it," Mike smiled. "But the source of some of his money was a problem." As Adele looked at him expectantly, Mercutio added, "He owns the biggest casino in the Midwest."

Adele sat back in her chair and stiffened, exhibiting her surprise and embarrassment that it had never occurred to her that there would be an American Indian entrepreneur of great wealth who would be interested in pro sports ownership. She had grown up in an area where the federal policy had given reservations the right to operate full-fledged, Las Vegas type casinos on tribal land. At first, the considerable wealth resulting had universally been held communally by the band or tribe. As groups of native Americans broke out of the appalling poverty that had held them back, Adele had not been surprised that individual entrepreneurs would emerge. However she had not anticipated that casino ownership itself would be within the portfolios of individual Native Americans.

"I thought any connection between professional football and gambling was an absolute prohibition," Adele said looking askance.

"Oh, it is," Mike said with certainty. "Greywolf agreed to put the casino into a blind trust so that it wouldn't prevent his eligibility to own a pro football team. Even at that, it was a pretty big give on the part of the league office and the other owners not to insist that he sell the casino rather than simply divorce himself from its operation. But ethnic minority ownership in any pro sport is a rarity and is so highly desired as a positive public image for the professional sport that an accommodation was considered worthwhile. Once Greywolf distanced himself from the casino, his other considerable assets made him a very well-funded bidder for the franchise."

Adele toyed with her empty coffee cup and moved on to fingering her silverware for a time before she spoke. "So there appears to be no financial connection between Senator Brockhurst and the Loggers ownership. And, with the casino in a blind trust, Greywolf isn't slipping money to Brockhurst because he has no need to buy his support."

"That's how it is, Adele," Mike said with an openhanded gesture. "Brockhurst probably backed the franchise effort and stadium effort because those developments were popular with the voters."

Adele nodded agreement because she could neither think of a relevant question or a comment that might open a different line of exploration. With the journalistic aspect of the lunch meeting concluded, Mike turned to asking her a series of questions that revealed his obvious interest in wanting to know her better. Adele found his interest pleasant and somewhat flattering. Mike's queries were not overly personal and focused on areas of interest that they shared. She lingered much longer than had been her intention. She was not surprised when Mike proposed they have dinner that evening. She had obligations and had to decline. When his inquiry about the next evening, his last in town, also had to be declined, she agreed that if his work required him to stay an unexpected third day, she would dine with him.

Later, in the spartanly furnished room that passed for a break room for Sentinel employees, Adele and Abe sat facing one another across the scarred and stained table that bore the effects of innumerable cigarette burns and coffee spills. Abe shoved to one side the cup of cold coffee he had long since abandoned. "So we got no help there," he concluded after Adele had reported what Mike Mercutio had told her at lunch.

"Makes you wonder if Penelope Dayton was kidding herself that she had something sensational to sell," said Adele.

Abe shook his head from side to side. "I'd guess people in her line of work are pretty realistic. We just haven't hit on a lead into the story yet."

Adele shrugged her shoulders. "Maybe we've had a lead that's so subtle that we just haven't recognized it."

Abe felt so stymied that he suppressed a playful retort suggesting that Adele must have been too distracted at lunch to grasp the implications of what her handsome lunch host had said. "Let's go over it again. There is no indication that Brockhurst profited by helping Greywolf's group acquire the football franchise or get the new stadium. Yet Harold Fortner, a major league campaign consultant, is here working on the mere possibility of a dark horse campaign. And Fortner says that money isn't a problem for Brockhurst, an aspirant with only a regional reputation from a low clout state with little fundraising potential. Does that lead to any speculation about what the story was that Penelope Dayton wanted to sell?"

Adele shrugged again and offered, "She knew where the money was coming from?"

"Perhaps not just *where* it was coming from but that the *where* isn't legit," Abe proposed.

Adele frowned, "You think that someone would be dumb enough to tell her that?"

"Not dumb, but arrogant and unguarded in the afterglow of passion, perhaps?" Abe asked cynically.

Adele smiled disingenuously. "That's outside my area of expertise."

"I'm glad to hear it," Abe said with sincerity than was perhaps too emphatic. "You think we could find out where Brockhurst's money comes from?"

"Wait," Adele said and paused in thought. "I've been making an assumption that may not be true."

"Which is what exactly?"

"I have assumed that Brockhurst wouldn't be using his personal fortune for this campaign. What if he's planning to use his personal fortune for this campaign?"

"I'd be surprised if that's the case," Abe mused. "Brockhurst has a substantial personal fortune, but surely he wouldn't bankrupt himself for a long shot political effort."

"That depends on how badly he wants it, doesn't it?" Adele suggested. "He wouldn't be the first person with deep pockets to spend a big chunk of his own money to run for political office."

"If he did that," Abe reasoned, "there'd be not story of an inappropriate or embarrassing nature to hide. Everyone knows where the family money came from."

"The sale of the family business is well known, but what do we know about his finances since then?" Adele considered. "Maybe he has a blind trust like Sam Greywolf does, of maybe he's done something more hands on. We really should check out his personal finances to the extent that public records will show."

Abe nodded agreement. "Also, like any incumbent politician, he has carry over campaign funding from previous campaigns where it was not expended. We should find out how much of that there is."

"Why don't you find out what the size of Brockhurst's campaign fund is. Since it can't ultimately be confidential, the question shouldn't be objectionable?" Adele suggested.

"And you're going to tackle his personal finances?" Abe asked.

"Yes."

"Maybe I should do that," Abe offered.

"Why?"

"There could be a hostile response to that inquiry," Abe said.

"Hey, I can handle anything you can handle," Adele huffed. "I'll take the finances assignment."

"Come on, Adele. Let's switch assignments."

"No we won't," Adele decreed, "I'm on it." With a air of finality, she sailed out of the room.

Chapter

21

The rules on the disclosure of funds expended by a candidate (as separate from those spent by so-called separate support groups) in campaigning for political office obviously could not be fully disclosed until the end of the campaign. Of greater relevance to Abe's attempt to examine Senator Brockhurst's political war chest was that he had not even declared his candidacy yet. Therefore, the senator was not yet under obligation to report anything, even in the voluntary sense of disclosing the expenditures of a so-called exploratory effort to decide whether or not to run. However, like other elected officials who had been through several re-election efforts, Brockhurst had funds that he had carried over from previous campaigns. Such amounts grew increasingly substantial as an incumbent faced weaker and weaker opposition as the likelihood of an opponent unseating him or her lessened.

Thus, it would not be surprising to be told that Brockhurst was holding an amount that would fund the sort of exploratory effort to test whether or not interest in a serious campaign could be ignited. Abe's initial inquiry was a straightforward task. He would simply call the Senator's office in the federal building in downtown Pauliapolis and ask the senator's chief of staff what was the amount of the senator's senatorial re-election fund. It was a question that the senator's office could, by law or common sense, decline to answer. That fact not withstanding, it took him several phone calls over the course of the afternoon to get an answer to his question, first because it was claimed that the chief of staff was unavailable and later because that person, now being available, supposedly needed time to look up information to be certain that he was being entirely accurate. Abe recognized a ploy to gain the time for discussions to occur as to why an inquiry was being made at this time and for what presumed devious purpose.

When the senator's chief of staff, Mark Dryer, gave him the figure, Abe could not suppress a dubious reaction. "That's it? I thought it would be much higher. My guess would be that any third term senator across the country would report a figure about three times as large."

"Bear in mind the senator isn't up for re-election for four years," Dwyer said. "Besides, that's more than was spent in each one of the senator's previous re-election campaigns."

"It's barely enough for a bare bones exploration of a presidential run, let alone a campaign for the nomination," Abe challenged.

"Oh," Dwyer responded breathily, "if there is an exploration of a run for higher office, this money won't be touched for that or a nomination campaign. The senator will use his own resources for that."

Abe was slow to react as he absorbed what had been said. "His own resources, you say? You mean his personal assets?"

"Yes."

Abe was truly surprised. "I wasn't aware that the senator was a wealthy man—quite affluent certainly--but not wealthy," Abe mused.

"The senator has been a very successful investor," Dwyer said tersely.

"Yes?" Abe asked. "How successful?"

"You understand that there is no need for disclosure until personal money has been used in a campaign. You are aware that the senator hasn't even decided to announce yet. If he does, his expenditures are subject to disclosure, and you can be sure that he will comply fully. In fact, the question then will be whether or not other contenders will match the openness of his campaign."

Abe caught the smugness in Dwyer's voice. "Why stand on the technicality?" Abe asked. "Why not just give me a ball park figure now?"

"I'm not authorized. Besides, you've no right to ask."

Abe recognized that familiar point in an interview where the stone wall started. If the interviewee were someone Abe was unlikely to want to interview ever again, one might make an attempt to breach the wall. However, if one were likely to want to make inquiry of the source again, it was wiser not to risk annoying a subject who would turn uncommunicative ever afterward. Abe offered a pro forma thank you and cradled his phone.

Chapter

22

I t having been too late in the day to report to Adele the meager outcome of his interview with Brockhurst's chief of staff, Abe looked for her the next morning to bring her up to date. She had not yet arrived when he went by her cubicle. He got involved in his work and did not seek her again until early afternoon. When Abe asked the young copy writer in the cubicle adjoining Adele's if she had seen Adele, he was astonished to be told that Adele was in the hospital. Because the young woman did not know the cause Adele's being hospitalized or her condition, Abe rushed to Henry Burton's office to learn what the editor might know.

Burton answered his hastily expressed inquiry calmly. "She's not hurt real bad. She broke her wrist and skinned up her side painfully getting out of the way of a car that almost hit her."

"When did it happen?" Abe asked.

"Last night at about nine," Henry shook his head in disgust. "She had the green light and stepped off the curb. Apparently. she didn't see a car that was behind her that was making a right turn. Luckily she was able to jump back out of the way, but she tripped and broke her wrist easing her fall. She also scraped her thigh and shoulder on the sidewalk. The police say that the corner's not well lit. Technically, it was a hit-and-run but the police think that the driver never saw her, so he didn't stop. The hospital patched her up and kept her over night as a precaution. She seems to be O.K. except for the discomfort of her injuries."

Abe stared thoughtfully. "Are the cops sure it was an accident?"

"They seemed so," Burton said. He looked at Abe quizzically. "Why? Do you think it might be otherwise?"

Abe wished he had not asked. "No. My question was just the reporter coming out in me. Always suspicious."

Henry Burton looked unconvinced by Abe's hasty rationalization. Abe hastened to change the focus of the editor's attention. "What hospital's she in? How long is she going to be there? I should look in on her."

Burton stared searchingly at his reporter. Abe was not known for his solicitousness toward his colleagues. "She's at County General. They're letting her out this afternoon unless something unexpected turns up."

Abe was anxious to talk to Adele for several reasons, but mainly he wanted to assure himself that she was all right. "I'll see if she needs a ride home."

Everything Abe said seemed to make Burton look more suspicious. "Is something going on, Abe? You two aren't working on a story together, are you?"

"No," Abe said emphatically. "Unless you gave Adele an assignment for the two of us, and she hasn't had a chance to tell me yet."

"What made you think that her injury might not be an accident?" Burton pressed.

"These days, there's always the possibility of random, intentional violence," Abe offered. He turned toward the door.

"Abe," Burton called after him, "keep me posted." After a pause, Burton added, "About everything."

Abe nodded his acquiescence curtly and hurried on to phone the hospital to have them tell Adele that he would be there to pick her up shortly.

When he entered Adele's hospital room, she was just finishing combing her hair with slow, awkward left-handed strokes. Abe noted the cast on her right wrist. She saw him in the mirror and said, "Hey,

Abe, I'm just about ready to go." She put down the comb and started toward the nearby chair. Her cautious and awkward movements were quite unlike those that were normal for the former record-setting athlete. She winced a bit as she settled herself into the chair. "They're bringing a wheel chair."

"You look like you need it," Abe said.

"Actually, I'm fine. But the abrasions have scabbed over and they complain of movement that pulls at them. I could walk out, but the hospital has a rule."

"Don't be ridiculous; you're in no condition to walk to the car," Abe said with more vehemence than he intended. "I'll bring the car to the door and you can slide in from the wheel chair."

Adele smiled broadly. "No problem, doc. Whatever you say."

Abe felt a little embarrassed. "I just want you in shape to answer some questions and fill me in." At that point a nurse brought in a wheel chair and braked it in front of Adele.

"Yeh, we've got to talk," Adele answered as she shifted uncomfortably into the wheel chair. "But let it keep until I get settled in at home."

Abe nodded and left to get his car. The nurse slowly turned the wheel chair and began to push it and Adele toward the entrance where discharged patients are picked up.

When they reached Adele's small ranch house, the well-kept grounds of which showed the ravages of the end of fall and the frosts which the arrival of cold weather had brought. Abe was immediately distressed by Adele's painful hobble for the few steps she managed after she struggled with his assistance to get out of the car. He insisted Adele let him help, and she did not resist. Being careful to lift her into his arms with her injured right side away from him, he carried her up the walk and the few steps onto the small porch. He set her down at the front door. Adele said that Abe's assistance to that point had been more than sufficient and resisted further help as she struggled to open the door and made her way haltingly across the entry way and toward a reclining chair in the living room.

Abe trailed her into the room and took in his surroundings. Adele walked over to a recliner and turned to stand with her back to it. Then she backed up until the back of her calves touched the chair. She gritted her teeth and lowered herself into it. She smiled as she leaned back into a comfortable arrangement.

Abe took in the soft beige walls of the room. He noted that the off-white and pale blue furnishings harmonized attractively. An entertainment center just short of being too large for the room signaled that the resident enjoyed a range of diversions. Abe was tempted to examine the CD containers out of curiosity about Adele's musical taste, but he restrained himself for fear of being thought intrusive.

"Want me to make you some coffee or something?" he offered and looked to locate the entrance to the kitchen.

"Will you stop mothering me?" Adele said and smiled a tense, crooked smile. "On second thought," she said, "I could use a glass of water. Through there," she pointed.

Abe returned quickly and handed her the glassful of water. He sat in the chair nearest Adele's recliner and said, "Tell me what happened."

"I'm not really sure. The light turned green. I started to cross. I caught a glimpse of a car making a right turn right at me and I jumped back; I dove, really. The car didn't hit me, but I hit the concrete sidewalk and slid hard."

"Did you look back to your left before you started to cross?" Abe asked. "You know; to see if there was a car back there showing a turn signal."

"Abe," Adele sighed, "I thought I *had* looked. It would have been the normal thing to do, right? But I'm not certain. Maybe I did what the cops concluded. Walked out without looking."

"That doesn't sound like you," Abe muttered. His feelings about Adele would not admit to her being careless. "Maybe you looked and there was a dark colored car with no turn signal showing. In any case, the driver didn't stop to see if you were hurt."

"The police figure he didn't see me," Adele shrugged.

"A conclusion that saves them some trouble." Abe snorted. Responding to Adele's blank expression, he continued. "Their version doesn't require them to have to look for the driver in an unsuccessful hit-and-run attack, does it?"

Adele finished the water in the glass that Abe had brought her and said, "That's a bit melodramatic, isn't it?"

Abe hoped that Adele perceived his earnestness. "That depends on what you were doing yesterday."

Adele shifted about in the recliner in her ceaseless effort to find a comfortable position. "I was following up on the assignment that we'd agreed to. I checked out what public records show about Brockhurst's finances and found out very little."

"Don't tell me he has a blind trust like Greywolf?"

"Not a blind trust but a so-called family trust. If he wants to take a shot at the nomination with his own money and use everything, he could fund a robust effort."

"How robust?"

"Six hundred and forty-five million."

Abe grunted in surprise. "Wow. I didn't realize that he was so well off. How did he come by such wealth?"

"I couldn't find out if the total comes from anything besides the sale of the family business," Adele said as she winced and shifted position again, "I wasn't able to check out who bought his assets."

"So we've got nothing," Abe concluded and pressed his mouth into the crunch that signaled his frustration.

"Unless you found something," Adele responded.

"I didn't get anything either," Abe nodded. "The senator's office seems calm and confident. His chief of staff says that if he does run, money's not a problem. If he's willing to spend his own bucks, I guess it isn't."

"Of course, we don't really know if his business dealings are above board," Adele mused.

"You think he's been exploiting some widows and orphans?" Abe said, his frustration leading to a lack of seriousness.

"No," Adele said, drawing the word out to express impatience with Abe's loss of focus. "But, the secret that was spilled to Penelope Dayton may have to do with something questionable about the source of the senator's money. It couldn't hurt to look at that angle."

"Maybe it's already hurt to look at that angle," Abe asserted.

"I don't follow," Adele admitted.

If your almost getting run down yesterday wasn't an accident, it was because of what you were looking into," Abe proposed.

"You're making quite a leap, Abe. I didn't really find out anything damaging. Besides, if someone really had tried to run me down, wouldn't I have been more seriously hurt?"

"Maybe the driver wasn't good at his job. Or maybe the target's superior reflexes prevented the hit," Abe argued.

"I don't have the reflexes of a collegiate jock anymore, thank you, kind sir," Adele retorted, refusing to take Abe's reasoning seriously.

Abe stood and paced for a bit. "Try this as a scenario. Penelope Dayton's client Harold Fortner reveals to her in the afterglow of passion that he's got a live one as a long shot presidential possibility because his has a good record and a respected image and is surprisingly well funded. He, Harold the magical king maker, just may pull this long shot effort off because Brockhurst won't have the usual problem of candidates with insufficient funds being unable to hang in past the early winnowing, which is the point where the contenders are in the position to attract the money needed to stay in all the way to the convention.

"If Fortner's penchant to play the big man got the better of his judgment, he told the lovely lady that the gold is ill-gotten, though not obviously so. When it looks like the funny-money cat may get out of the bag, the first containment move got the potential leak out of town. Then, when the nosey press is still after the secret, the campaign wizard tries to dispose of that problem with the front end of his car."

Adele could not suppress a smile despite the discomfort of her injuries. "You realize there's not one confirmed fact in that whole scenario? We don't know for certain if Fortner was Dayton's client. We don't know--if he was her client--what, if anything, he told her. Assuming the truth of those two gigantic 'ifs,' we don't know if she over-estimated how damaging what she was told is. Finally, if she did know anything damaging, we don't know if we're close enough to knowing what it is that someone would try to get rid of us."

"One small correction," Abe said with raised finger. "They didn't try to get rid of 'us'; they tried to get rid of you. Have you found out something that you haven't had a chance to share with me?"

Adele shook her head negatively. "Nothing. I didn't find out anything other than what's public information about any politician."

"Maybe there's more to the money story than you were able to get by ethical means. I think it's my turn to go after the money angle of this story with some unconventional tactics."

"What are you going to do?" Adele asked. She raised the recliner to a sitting position and repeated with heightened emphasis, "What are you going to do, Abe?"

"I'm going to squeeze Harold Fortner a little bit. I'll pretend I know for certain what I only suspect and see if I can prompt him to say or do something foolish." He said it with the finality that conveyed an unwillingness for further discussion.

"Don't do it, Abe," Adele said firmly. "I'm sure it's occurred to you that, if Fortner is as dangerous as you suspect, you would become a target. We'll think of something else."

"There isn't anything else," Abe stated with firmness equal to Adele's. He turned to go and then stopped and faced Adele. "You going to be O.K. here alone? I could get someone from the paper to come and look after you."

"I'm going to be fine," Adele said. "You just make sure that you're the same."

"I should be so lucky that he'd actually threaten me," Abe said and waved a goodbye, leaving Adele sitting there looking concerned.

Chapter

23

Abe spent considerable time rehearsing series of questions that might tempt Harold Fortner into a response that hinted at the next step to uncovering the embarrassing secret connected to Senator Brockhurst's nascent presidential campaign. However, this planned application of his journalistic subtlety never occurred. When he called Senator Brockhurst's office to request an interview with the campaign consultant, he was informed that Fortner was out of town and had been so for several days.

Abe reported this to Adele when he came by her home in the late afternoon. He found her moving about with considerably more ease than he would have expected based on her condition the previous day. When Abe commented on her ease of movement, she explained that keeping the abrasions moist with the suave she had been provided gave her comfort of movement. Adele offered to make him a sandwich, which she was doing quite handily for herself despite the cast on her right wrist. He accepted her offer.

Abe sat on a kitchen stool admiring the fluidity of Adele's movements. She was, though injured, incapable of moving awkwardly. Her easy smile and relaxed face belied whatever pain she surely continued to feel. It now puzzled Abe that he had not noticed how admirable Adele is until a few weeks ago although they had been colleagues for over two years. As Adele set the sandwich before him, she said with some amusement, "So your theory that Fortner tried to run me down is totally shot."

"That doesn't mean that somebody didn't try it," Abe countered. "Or won't again. I'm going to have to keep an eye on you just in case."

"Whoa, Abe Fuller," Adele objected. "I'm in no need of a nursemaid, thank you." However, her smile told Abe that she was not displeased at his expression of concern.

"All I'm saying is that it's wise to be careful until we find out for sure that nothing dangerous is going on," Abe said solicitously. "It occurs to me that one thing we could do to check into whether something dangerous is going on is to talk to Penelope Dayton. She may have experienced something suspicious since you spoke to her. Even if she hasn't, she deserves a warning about possible danger and for us tell her what we suspect."

"What you suspect, you mean," Adele corrected. "But that's not a bad idea." Adele glanced at her watch. "I'll give her a call while you work on that sandwich."

As Adele headed for the phone in her study, Abe asked, "You have her phone number?"

"No, but I have her address. I can get it."

Abe was not half way through the sandwich when Adele returned with a frown on her face. "The number's been disconnected," she announced.

Abe matched Adele's frown. "It's not likely she'd go unlisted. She must have moved already. That should tell you something. You still think that I'm overly suspicious?"

"I don't know what to think," Adele said pensively.

"I still think I've got to work on Fortner," Abe concluded and went back to finishing his sandwich.

"You'll keep looking over your shoulder, won't you?" Adele asked.

"Not to worry," Abe said confidently as he followed the last bite of his sandwich with a swallow of coffee and reached for his coat. "I've got work to do. Call me if you need anything."

"I'm fine. I'll be in the office tomorrow."

Abe clasped Adele lightly by both shoulders. "These are two fine shoulders for looking over. Don't *you* forget to use them for that." He was tempted to kiss her on the cheek, but was unsure of how she would react to that, so he made his exit.

Getting an interview with Harold Fortner proved to be a little more difficult than Abe anticipated, although politicians running for office and their staffs sought rather than shunned publicity. The senator's chief of staff at first declined to schedule an interview for Abe with the senator's campaign consultant. The chief of staff insisted that the senator and not the advisor for a potential campaign which had not yet been decided on was the proper person for Abe to talk to. Abe argued that he intended to do a piece on contemporary approaches to campaigning. Since he would be writing on the how and the what of campaigns in general as they are now being done, Fortner was the right person for him to talk to. Abe stressed that his article would not be about any particular candidate and not about Brockhurst and his possible plans. The focus of the piece would be on the current milieu for managing a campaign; hence Fortner was the most knowledgeable person for him to talk to.

Abe received a call from Brockhurst's office later confirming a meeting time the next day for him to talk to Harold Fortner. The senator's chief of staff stressed the condition that the subject of the interview would be limited to the nature and dynamics of contemporary campaigning. Abe was told that Fortner now worked from within a small suite in a building across the street from the senator's office in the federal building.

In the morning, the political consultant was effusive and friendly as he invited Abe into his office. His amiable air was a marked contrast to the cautious demeanor Fortner had shown in attending Abe's recent interview with him. Fortner unbuttoned the coat of the well-cut navy blue suit he was wearing and settled into a leather wing chair as he pointed Abe to an identical chair across a low table that stood between them.

"I understand that you have some questions about the nuts and bolts of campaigning that you're doing a piece on," Fortner said as he clasped his palms together on his lap.

"Actually, I'm just exploring the possibility of a feature article on the how and why of the way that national campaigning is done currently. I feel that you know more about it than anyone else around here at the moment, so you're the starting point."

Fortner smiled the smile of a knowing veteran, "I've been involved in some big ones, it's true."

"Isn't it so that the kind of role you perform for people pursuing political office is a recent phenomenon in American politics?" Abe asked with notebook in hand.

Fortner extended his hand toward Abe with the palm vertical in a gesture of caution. "Wait. This article wouldn't be about me, would it? If that's what you have in mind, we won't be proceeding. Someone who does the kind of the work I do wants to have as low profile as possible. In my business, it's never about us; it's always about the candidate. That should be obvious."

"But isn't it true that in some instances a campaign advisor has literally created a new persona for the candidate and decided the issues that the candidate should emphasize or avoid?"

Fortner revealed a smugness that he seemed to struggle against unsuccessfully. "It's a consultant's job to maximize his candidate's--his employer, don't forget--chances of success."

"Even if it means convincing him or her to behave contrary to the habits of a lifetime, his inborn personality traits and his previously articulated principles?"

Fortner shook his head from side to side in response. "That's a fiction promulgated by the media. What you've just described can't be done, even if a candidate would be willing to submit to it. Some things about the factors you mentioned can be tweaked a little to give the public what they think they want. That's the extent of it."

"How much is a tweak?" Abe asked, his own smile escaping him to reveal more than he wished.

Fortner laughed heartily. "An interesting but unanswerable question."

"What's more tweakable, the candidate's personal image or his or her stand on the issues?" Abe asked with an unabashedly cynical smile.

"Issue positions are definitely more malleable, especially if the candidate is a relative unknown and people aren't quite sure where he stood to begin with," Fortner offered confidently. "Of course, unknowns are also easier to shape an image for, since the public doesn't already have a fixed perception."

"That makes it seem as though it's an advantage to be an unknown rather than an established figure," Abe concluded. He hoped he could steer Fortner to the subject of Brockhurst's situation by implication rather than direct questions.

"That's frequently the case," Fortner nodded. "Except that unknowns almost always lack the funds to make themselves known. It takes a lot of money to make oneself and one's positions known to the voters who will decide the race in question."

"I suppose that's why we're seeing an increase of newcomers to politics who have their own money to spend," Abe said.

Fortner spread his arms palms up to indicate his concurrence. "It's the only way to start for the person who hasn't been a career politician if he or she suddenly gets the itch to hold public office," Fortner said approaching lecturer mode. "However, the need for ample funding is just as crucial for the career politician who's contemplating a move up the political ladder."

"Certainly necessary for someone who's contemplating getting to the very top of the ladder," Abe asserted. "I understand from Senator Brockhurst's chief of staff that he is amply funded if he chooses to reach for the highest rung of the ladder."

Fortner appraised Abe calmly. "Actually, the senator and I haven't talked about resources yet. I can assure you that my consultant's fees for the exploratory effort, which are quite substantial, were paid up front. I don't work on any other basis."

"Up to now the senator's not shown, nor has he needed, extremely deep pockets," Abe said equally calmly. "Aren't you at least curious about his funding? After all, this upcoming campaign is such a wide open situation in both major parties. With no incumbent and no dominating front runners, someone in your business would want to hook up with an aspirant who has the resources to stay the course and run a strong campaign."

Fortner shifted in his chair and showed the slightest bit of tension in his posture. "You forget the ground rules on which this interview was granted. I agreed to talk about campaigning in general, not the senator's situation in particular."

"I asked my question improperly," Abe said contritely. "What I meant is that a professional campaigner has to make choices among potential clients. That's especially true for one who's been as successful as you. Surely, the availability of funds must be among the first factors in making that choice of clients. I just assumed that one would establish how much money a potential client has to use and where it comes from. Surely that would be the first consideration before one chooses a client."

"Why would I be interested in where the money comes from?" Fortner asked and then held up his hand to signal a withdrawal of his question. "Let me re-phrase that. The source of funds isn't a consultant's concern."

"Doesn't that leave the door open for potential embarrassment down the road?" Abe asked with as innocent an air as he could muster.

"That wouldn't be my--that is, the consultant's--embarrassment, would it?" Fortner injected with the most defensiveness that he had shown so far. "A consultant can't be expected to be an ethical watchdog, can he?"

"No, I guess not," Abe responded with furrowed brow, unable to completely hide his lack of conviction. He paused over his notes with no purpose other than the hope that the tension between him and Fortner might increase.

Fortner looked at his watch, and said, "Can we wind this up? I'm just about out of time."

Abe smiled despite the failure of his ploy. He had pursued his purpose as far as he felt he could. Unfortunately, Fortner had not given any hint of an impropriety in Brockhurst's campaign situation of which the political consultant had become aware and perhaps revealed to Penelope Dayton. If he had revealed anything during a dalliance with his former playmate, he had become more guarded and was not about to repeat his mistake by revealing it to a journalist.

Of course, it still was possible that Fortner's avoidance of the subject of the source of campaign funding was itself a signal of something improper lurking. Abe was not convinced that the eventual implosion of a campaign because of financial impropriety would not produce a damaging reflection on the professional staff, but he was in no position to press the argument. He closed his notebook resignedly. "Actually, I don't have anything else." He stood and extended his hand toward Fortner. "Thank you for your time. You've been very helpful."

Beyond the pro forma expression of gratitude, Abe remained hopeful that Fortner's statements might actually have been helpful for a somewhat different purpose than the political consultant might suppose.

Chapter

24

Abe restrained himself throughout the late afternoon and evening from calling Adele to report the outcome of his interview with Fortner. Of course, he really had nothing meaningful to report, but he enjoyed Adele's company and wanted to talk to her. Besides, he wanted a report on her recuperation from her accident. So he repeatedly reached for the phone, hoping that she would invite him for further discussion of their investigation. However, he stopped short of using the phone. She needed to rest, he reasoned, especially if she insisted on returning to work the next day.

Furthermore, perhaps he checked himself because he suspected he was becoming too fond of Adele's company. That would be a problem if his frequent presence was unwanted. Besides, not getting involved was the surest prevention of rejection. It was a rule he had lived by since the one great romantic disappointment of his life. He sometimes wondered if he had erred in extending the rule to mere feminine friendship as well. The truth was that he did not hunger for friendship in general. Adele might be the exception. Nevertheless, he spent the rest of the day restlessly making notes for a piece on the special pro football draft in which the Loggers could choose from a list to which each of the established teams had been obliged to contribute. But the draft was still several months off, and he could not concentrate on speculating who might be on the list that the Loggers would be interested in. His mind kept straying to wondering why Adele was not curious enough about his meeting with Fortner to call him and ask how it had gone. That question dominated his thoughts until bedtime.

The next morning, he did call Adele as early as he dared to offer her a ride to work and found that she had already left home. When he got to the Sentinel building, he went directly to Adele's cubicle and found it empty. It was surprising that she had not arrived yet, he thought, since her distance from home to the office was no farther than he own. He walked through the surrounding cubicles asking if anyone had seen her and found no one who had. His concern that her injury of two days previous had not been an accident was re-awakened, and he wondered if she had carelessly risked her safety again.

He was pondering where to continue his search for her when he saw her emerge from the elevator and wave at him as he stood near her cubicle. Abe asked where she had been with enough vehemence that Adele frowned at him in surprise. "What's wrong?" she asked.

"Nothing," Abe responded sheepishly. "I knew you were coming in today, but I couldn't find you. I knew you'd left home and no one around here had seen you."

Adele smiled. "What? You thought I'd stepped in front of another car?" Abe felt his face flush. "Come on, Abe, there's nothing to worry about. Let's get some coffee. I want to hear about your meeting with Fortner. And then I've got something to tell you."

They sat on opposite sides of a worn table sipping coffee in the spartanly furnished room that served as an employees' lounge for that floor of the building. Abe briefly summarized his encounter with Harold Fortner, concluding that Fortner had not let anything revealing slip out in his responses to Abe's questions. "Unless, of course, his refusal to talk about money confirms the possibility that the story's about money."

Adele nodded affirmatively. "Let me tell you what I learned about the money angle."

Abe shook his head, again impressed with Adele's skill at

investigation. "How were you able from home to do any digging beyond the surface of the situation?"

"I wasn't," Adele conceded. "I just talked to Joel Harrison this morning about the obvious."

"The guy who writes the business news?" Abe asked doubtfully.

"Yes, him," Adele said a bit smugly. "Everything he got for me is from the public record. But before I get to that, here's a fact. Sam Greywolf has never given a campaign contribution, not so much as a dime, to Senator Brockhurst."

"So what?" Abe snorted.

Adele frowned at Abe's failure to grasp the implications of the fact and explained. "The senator had been very influential in the city's getting not only an NFL franchise of which Greywolf is controlling owner but also a new stadium for Greywolf's team to play in. However, Greywolf hasn't ever given the helpful senator even an entirely legal contribution?" Adele expostulated.

"Hey, Adele, be careful," Abe said with a smile. "Next you'll be quoting that secretary of defense of a few years back who said that the absence of any evidence that a thing exists is the very evidence proving that the thing probably does exist. We can't really join the 'there's no evidence of his innocence so he must be guilty' thinkers, can we?"

"I can't fight your logic, Abe; I'm just saying it's odd. Fanatic football fans would think that Greywolf's showing his appreciation is obligatory and even voters who aren't fans would find it unsurprising if he helped the senator in an acceptable way," Adele argued.

"O.K., my gut as a reporter wants to agree with you," Abe admitted.

"Now, here's what Harrison told me about Brockhurst," Adele said. "He sold the family company about a year ago."

"That is old news, Adele; you took me through that before. The family trust, etc.," Abe said.

"I'm glad your memory's fine, Abe, but the details are revealing. Brockhurst inherited a little forest products manufacturing business from his father. He focused it on making quality hardwood veneer paneling: oak, maple, cherry, even imported exotic woods. He did very well, much better than his father."

"So he sold his empire," Abe stated. "What's the point?"

"He got six hundred million."

"Hence," Abe nodded. "It's no wonder his chief of staff says money won't be a problem if Brockhurst runs. Still nothing startling."

Adele smiled a bit smugly. "What makes the sale interesting, Joel says, is that the most recent appraisal places the value of Brockhurst's former company at a little over two hundred million."

"He really found himself a sucker, or to be kind, a generous buyer," Abe said, shaking his head at the irrationality. "Let me guess," he said with a knowing smirk, "The buyer was Sam Greywolf."

"Don't you wish," Adele offered wryly. "It was some holding company called "Omni Enterprises."

"Could Joel find out anything about Omni?"

"Nothing of interest to us. Omni owns a variety of businesses. Nothing among the other companies they own links to Brockhurst," Adele said resignedly. "It looks like we've at a dead end. I wouldn't know where to go from here to look for something improper. Maybe there isn't anything."

"Maybe," Abe shrugged. "On the other hand, unless the company tanked in the last year, the senator's receiving three times the company's value a year ago is suspicious. That generosity would be the something that Penelope Dayton knew that she thought was worth twenty-five thousand to make known."

"Well, we'll never get at it, it seems," Adele said as the telephone on a nearby shelf rang. She lifted the receiver and said, "Yes? He's right here. Of course. Right away." Adele replaced the receiver and looked at Abe with raised eyebrows. "Henry Burton wants to see us."

"Both of us?"

"Right now, it seems." Addle said and stood. "And he sounded rather firm about it."

"Now what?" Abe wondered as he followed Adele out of the room.

The answer to Abe's question was not long in coming after they seated themselves before the editor. Burton peered at them across his desk and asked, "Just what have you two been up to?" The pair could offer no response other than a puzzled expression. Burton looked impatient. "Are you guys going to pretend you have no idea why I asked you here?"

"We're not pretending," Adele said as they both shook their heads in a joint display of their not being able to respond the editor's question.

Burton furrowed his forehead resignedly. "I keep forgetting. Bluntness is the only way to reach either of you two." Burton looked sharply at the pair. He spoke with a lowered and measured the tone to his voice as he pronounced, "Mr. Etheridge has had a call from his good friend Senator Brockhurst. It seems that the senator is unhappy that a couple of Mr. Etheridge's reporters are working overtime to throw a wrench into the senator's presidential aspirations. I don't recall making any assignment for either one of you to do anything remotely on that order."

Both reporters hastened to begin a protest at an unwarranted accusation. Because their competing voices made them both incomprehensible to the editor, he raised his hand to silence them. "You first," Burton said pointing to Abe.

"There's nothing remotely like a smear about anything that we've looked into, Henry." Abe quickly summarized their investigation and its results since Penelope Dayton had disappeared rather than accept the paper's offer to pay twenty-five thousand dollars for her story. Abe made himself the very picture of candor and contriteness as he said, "That's where it stands, chief. If there's any heat to be taken for following up on the Dayton thing, I accept it. I shouldn't have gotten Adele to help me with my investigation."

"Whoa, whoa, whoa," Adele burst in, "what do you mean 'your' investigation? Who made the trip to L.A. to get things going? I'm the one whose story it is." Turning to Abe, she added, "I'm a big girl. I don't need anyone to cover for me."

"You went to L.A.?" Burton asked with elaborate but feigned amiability. "You apply for reimbursement on that?"

To Adele's negative nod, Abe added, "See, she went to help with my story. I'm going to reimburse her. I just haven't gotten around to it yet." Adele reacted with an astonished gasp.

Burton looked at the pair with growing impatience. "Will you two stop acting like a couple of high school sweethearts trying to cover for one another with the high school principal?"

Abe stole a sideways glance at Adele and saw that her face was as red as his felt. Looking back toward Burton, he saw that the man appeared to be amused at their discomfiture. Abe was surprised himself at how spontaneously he had leaped in to protect Adele from blame. Burton's description of them as high school sweethearts stayed with him. To his surprise, he felt quite comfortable with it.

"Now if we could be grownup journalists for a minute," Burton began, "I'm told that you don't have anything you could write about Brockhurst except a couple wild inferences that would injure a dedicated and loyal public servant."

Adele offered coolly. "Don't someone's paying three times what it's worth for the Brockhurst family business made drawing inferences irresistible?"

"Not necessarily of the sort that a responsible journalist would print," Burton asserted. He was silent for a while, studying his two reporters as though they were a neighbor's inconvenient and unattractive pets who had wandered into his yard. "What you have— if it's true and as yet not rebutted--is just the right amount information to overcome the owner's annoyance with you."

"That would be a great relief, chief," Abe said appreciatively.

"So the money angle's what we focus on?" Adele asked with an air of innocence that caused Abe to turn and stare at her.

"No-o," Burton said drawing the word out to give emphasis to his impatience. "Neither one of you will go anywhere near this story unless I tell you that you can; is that clear?"

Abe and Adele affirmed their understanding emphatically and exited the editor's office. After the door closed behind them, Adele said out of the side of her mouth solely the word, "Wimp."

Abe almost rose to the bait until he looked at his grinning colleague. "The phrase 'bull in a china shop' comes to mind, but of course you don't qualify physically."

"Yeh, and you're glad about that," Adele responded and punched Abe on the shoulder. He reacted with a friendly push, and they continued in a similar mode of verbal exchange and physical contact that was too juvenile to qualify for the high school age behavior of which Henry Burton had accused them.

Chapter

25

Abe Fuller never asked himself why he continued to spend so much time with Adele Friedman after they were no longer working together on a story. Without planning, their coffee breaks seemed to occur at the same time. Their conversations were always shop talk and, to Abe's surprise, quite relaxed and engaging. As a rule, he avoided talking sports with anyone because he was unnerved by the level of specious expertise that most fans were prone to express. His own view of sport was simple. There was a contest in which one individual or team succeeded and the other failed. While he did not deny that tactics and psychological factors could affect outcomes at times, he found arcane explanations of plays and attributions of near supernatural skill to players and genius to successful coaches as absurd.

In Adele, he found someone who shared his own enthusiasm and notion of sport. It also added to the ease of their conversations to be able to be blunt in his political opinions. If she did not agree, she did not take offense. With her, he re-gained the interest that he had had during the time that politics had been the subject he covered as a reporter and columnist.

If you had told Abe that he and Adele had had dates, he would have denied it. The several times he had taken her to dinner were necessitated by the continuation of one of their unfinished discussions. Adele, he was certain, would have agreed that these were not dates. They had become friends. That friendship explained why Abe, was concerned that Adele would have trouble getting to work on the day when the city had awakened to the first heavy snowfall of the season. He called Adele to tell her he would be by to take her to work and that he would come early enough to shovel her walk before they had to start for the office. Abe would have claimed that their friendship further explained why Adele told him that a substantial breakfast would be ready for him when he arrived. Friendship further explained why they shoveled together and had behaved more like youngsters at play than adults executing a chore before going to work.

Later that morning they were twenty minutes into a ten minute coffee break when Abe answered the phone in the lounge. Henry Burton, having recognized Abe's voice, asked if Adele was there with him. When Abe answered affirmatively, Burton said blandly, "There's a surprise. However, it does save the two of you a trip to my office. I have an assignment for the pair of you. Harold Fortner was killed in a car accident last night. Check it out."

"Was it a pedestrian accident?" Abe asked, quickly inferring a connection to his suspicion of Adele's having been nearly run down intentionally.

"No, I do know he was driving a car. Anything more than that," Burton said before pausing and adding sarcastically, "I was hoping you might find out for me." The editor cut off abruptly. Abe told his surprised colleague what their assignment was, and they set off to pursue the story of the political consultant's sudden demise.

From the highway patrol, they obtained a copy of the accident report. During the previous night's snowfall, Fortner was driving to the Pauliapolis airport to take a night flight to his Washington D.C. office. He had apparently lost control of his car exiting an underpass which not only went under a railroad bridge but also turned sharply after passing under the tracks. The highway patrol could not find any factor other than the weather conditions to account for the accident. They concluded that Fortner, who was the resident of a warmer part of the country, was unfamiliar with the driving adjustments necessitated to handle the poor visibility and the slippery conditions of the heavily falling snow. Since many lifelong residents of the northern climate lost control of their vehicles in circumstances like the previous night's conditions, the highway patrol did not find it unusual that someone unfamiliar with conditions of heavy snow and strong wind had lost control of his car. Though it was estimated that a half hour had elapsed before the wreck was found, the interval was not a factor in Fortner's death, which had been ruled instantaneous in the course of the car's rolling over and striking a tree.

The body had been moved to the city morgue pending an official identification of the body by Fortner's executive assistant, who was coming from Washington to identify the body and arrange for its removal to Washington.

Adele and Abe wondered why the identification could not be made by the senator or a member of his staff. When they decided to ask that question of Brockhurst's office, they were told that the authorities preferred the official identification be done by someone of longer and more intimate acquaintance that his current employer. When they asked if they might have a statement from the senator, they were told the senator was so stunned that he was unavailable, but that he would later fax the Sentinel his official statement of regret.

Realizing that Fortner's Washington colleague was, under the circumstances, their sole remaining source, the reporters asked if the senator's staff knew the Fortner's associate and how to reach him or her. They were told that Carl La Plante, Fortner's associate, would that afternoon be clearing Fortner's possessions from the apartment Fortner rented for his stay in Pauliapolis.

To prevent missing connections with La Plante, the reporters immediately went to the apartment building where Fortner had resided and waited a little over two hours before they saw a man approach the security guard's desk, identify himself, and ask for access to Fortner's apartment. They approached La Plante and identified themselves and asked if they might ask him some questions while he performed his task. He initial reluctance was overcome by pleading that there was surely going to be coverage in the national press of his colleague's death and that he should help them do a story for the local paper that would be more than the generalities of the wire services story.

Inside Fortner's apartment, Abe and Adele stood in the center of the living room while La Plante moved about the unfamiliar space gathering together what appeared to him as Fortner's personal effects for placement in the boxes that the building manager had promised to provide shortly. Adele asked, "Could you give us some insight into Fortner the man, that is the private side rather than the sought-after political operative?"

Abe felt a moment's impatience, thinking that Adele was leading the questioning away from he chance explore whether there was a suspicious element to Fortner's fatal accident. After a moment's additional thought, his realized the wisdom of her indirect approach. Alarming the stranger with the possibility of a crime might make him unresponsive.

La Plante stopped and was still for a moment. He shook his head from side to side and started toward a chair to sit down. He motioned the reporters toward the couch. "The personal side?" he said with a half smile on one side of his mouth. "There wasn't any personal side. His work was everything to him. He lived it all his waking hours, and if you were ever around him during a close campaign, there were nothing *but* waking hours."

"You sound like you admired him," Adele said.

"He had no equal at what he did," La Plante said firmly. "But he was a bit ruthless."

Abe offered. "It's a ruthless business."

"True enough," La Plante said without enthusiasm and seemed to wander from the present. "And admittedly his penchant going for the jugular was not the least among the qualities that made him so successful. However I think he had other more admirable skills. No one was better at analyzing polling data, or constructing the right sample for a poll or constructing a poll, for that matter. He had no equal in identifying which issues counted for a particular contest. And his perception for showing his client in the best possible light was uncanny. We've worked with candidates who thought he was crazy about the image he wanted them to project and later came to treat him almost reverently at the end of a successful campaign."

"You think he could have worked his magic for Senator Brockhurst?" Adele and Abe asked almost simultaneously. They turned to one another and shared a mutual satisfaction that they both had independently decided to turn the interview nearer to their concerns.

"I don't know," La Plante admitted, "but he was genuinely interested in the possibility of doing this campaign."

"Was his visit to the Washington office this weekend about definitely committing to a Brockhurst campaign?" Abe asked.

"We had no idea Harold was headed for the home office this weekend," La Plante said with a shrug.

"Perhaps he left a message or talked to another member of the staff in Washington," Adele offered.

"If he'd talked to anyone, that person would have told me. Harold was a stickler for coordination. And I checked for any message. He must have decided at the spur of the moment after the office was closed, and it wasn't urgent enough for him to call me at home," La Plante reasoned.

"He did have a bag in the car, didn't he?" Abe asked.

"Oh, yes," La Plante nodded. "And he had called in a plane reservation."

"I suppose you have looked through the bag?" Abe asked, "and it was his stuff." When La Plante responded affirmatively and showed a twitch of the lips like a suppressed smile, Abe followed up. "Was there something unusual about the contents of his bag?"

"Not so much unusual as surprising," La Plante answered. "He had packed underwear suitable for the cold weather you have around here that you wouldn't use in Washington unless the cold snap of the century was occurring. You guys acculturated him very quickly."

"Maybe they were for the trip back," Adele offered. "This climate makes you cautious about the weather. It can be deadly." Adele appraised La Plante's face for further reaction. "Was there anything else about what he was bringing along that surprised you?"

"Actually, something that he wasn't bringing was a little surprising," La Plante said, looking unsure that he was raising a matter of any significance.

"And what was that?" Abe prodded.

"His lap top wasn't in the car. It's right over there," La Plante said as he pointed toward the dining area that adjoined the living room.

"Maybe he had everything he needed for such a short trip in his brief case," Adele suggested.

"Harold didn't even own a brief case," La Plante said. "He considered them an annoyance, an impediment that encouraged avoidable weight that was easily prevented by having everything, and I do mean everything, on his computer. He used to joke that, if he could get the three of us on his permanent staff into the computer, it would be all of the office he needed. He never traveled without it."

"He could have decided on the trip so impulsively that he just forgot the lap top," Abe suggested.

"It would have been the first time," La Plante responded, "and I've been with him on the campaign trail where changes of travel plans were a daily occurrence."

"I've only got one more question," Abe said. He turned to Adele and offered, "Why don't you get to your other questions in before I finish."

"I don't have anything else," Adele said looking pleased at where the interview stood. "Go ahead and finish up."

"Had Mr. Fortner told you whether or not Senator Brockhurst had made the decision to run or whether he was going to manage the campaign if the senator did run?"

La Plante shook his head slowly, looking past his listeners with a mixture of sadness and frustration. "He hadn't said anything to indicate that the senator was near a decision one way or another, but I know he was quite interested in handling the campaign if it did happen. If the senator does run, those of us still remaining from Harold's firm will try to sell ourselves to him, but without Harold, it's going to be tough. He is—or was--the reigning guru of political campaigning."

The two reporters exchanged glances and stood to go. Adele approached La Plante and offered her hand. "We wish you well with your efforts to keep the firm going, Mr. La Plante. And please do accept our condolences on your loss." Adele shook La Plante's hand and Abe followed quickly on his colleague's lead, sharing the sense of closure she seemed to feel. They turned and exited without delay, careful not to display the curiosity that Fortner's associate would surely have found inappropriate rather than the solemnity that he himself was no doubt feeling.

As they strode toward the elevator, Adele looked at Abe challengingly and said, "I suppose you think Fortner was murdered."

"Oh, and I suppose you don't?" Abe responded guardedly.

Adele was unequal to continuing her feigned contrariness and nodded affirmatively, "A suspicious death, to say the least."

As they stepped into the elevator, Abe said, "There are the nagging little questions that Henry Burton would no doubt bring up if we tell him our suspicions: who and why?"

Adele did not hesitate in answering. "We've been flirting with a 'why' ever since we started into this fog. Fortner knew something that would at least embarrass, or even sink, Senator Brockhurst's bid for his party's presidential nomination," Adele offered.

"That's a reason to pay him a big fee to run the campaign, not kill him," Abe reasoned.

"Maybe he could not be counted on to keep quiet about it." Adele said.

"Or," Abe mused, "he was growing a mite too expensive to be kept silent."

"Being blackmailed would certainly would give Brockhurst a motive and a sense of urgency," Adele said as they exited the elevator and started through the lobby.

"That's a strong motive, O.K.," Abe agreed as he held the door open for Adele, "but it's not stronger than the one of the people who paid our good senator an indecently large amount of money for his family business."

"I don't see it. Making a bad deal is hardly a crime," Adele said.

"Maybe Omni was expecting to get more out of the deal than the company they bought."

"Like what?" Adele asked.

"How about a close connection to the most powerful man in the world?" Abe offered.

"Kind of a stretch," Adele said doubtfully. "Even if Brockhurst got his party's nomination, he'd still be a long way from the White House. The other party has deeper pockets and a couple of potentially more salable candidates."

"So," Abe said as he stopped in the cold afternoon air of Pauliapolis and concluded, "we're not ready to go back to Henry with anything. But we're agreed that Fortner's death is suspicious. We've got two suspects to check out: the senator and his minions and the Omni organization. Take your pick."

"I'll take the senator, his staff and his close friends," Adele said.

Abe nodded, "Good. I prefer to look at Omni anyway."

"I'll get started," Adele said and began to walk away.

"Not so fast," Abe said and took her arm. "First you take the pledge."

"What are you talking about?" Adele said with evident perplexity.

"You will be cautious. You will take no chances. You will not annoy dangerous people." Abe punctuated the statements with a serious tone.

"Hey," Adele said as she pulled his hand off her arm and squeezed it for a moment, "practice what you preach."

Abe watched her walk away and wondered if he should have suggested they investigate together rather than separately.

Chapter

26

A be provided Joel Harrison, the Sentinel's business columnist, with his day's amusement because the sports journalist did not know how or where to access on the internet the information available about publicly traded corporations. Harrison enjoyed having to lead Abe, in accompaniment with playful derision, through the labyrinth to find the list of all the companies held by Omni Enterprises.

Abe asserted in rebuttal that Harrison would experience similar problems to what Abe was experiencing if he tried to access sports information. This assertion proved to be a poor choice of rebuttal because Harrison, a lifelong fan of the Pauliapolis minor league baseball team in addition to being an inexplicably loyal Chicago Cubs fan, quickly tapped his way through a considerable array of baseball information until Abe was suitably humbled.

Abe pored over the printed out list of Omni's holdings for fifteen minutes before Harrison could no longer restrain himself and asked what Abe was looking for. "I don't exactly know what I'm looking for, if anything," Abe admitted. "This outfit Omni bought Senator Brockhurst's family company a year ago at what appears to be a very inflated price, and I wondered if there is something about Omni's other holdings that explains their interest in a wood products company."

"You can't always find a relatedness in the overall set of holdings of a company like Omni, Abe," Joel advised. "The companies in their portfolio don't necessarily have anything in common. In fact, they might have been chosen because they are diverse. Strangely enough, a conglomerate might even acquire some company because it needed to take a loss for tax purposes."

"You think maybe that's why Omni bought Brockhurst's wood products company?" Abe asked.

"That wasn't the talk at the time," Joel nodded. "You may not know that Brockhurst's former business has the most modern plant in the U.S. for the production of veneer paneling. Before it was acquired by Omni, it operated way under capacity. Omni said at the time that if they ran it full blast that they'd make much more money than Brockhurst did. They have operated at capacity for a while, but the profitability hasn't happened yet. A little more time will tell if they overpaid, unless the tax write off still makes the acquisition worth it."

"Maybe there's another reason for their interest," Abe mused, returning to his examination of the list of Omni's holdings.

"Let me see that thing," Joel asked, taking the sheet of paper from Abe's hand. After a minute's examination of the list, he said, "I don't see how it's relevant, but one of the other companies they own does business in the state."

"Which one's that?"

Harrison pointed to a line on the page. "Superior Management. It's a casino management company out of Las Vegas. They manage several casinos on the Indian Reservations in the state."

"Is one of them the Black River Casino on the Black River Reservation?" Abe asked.

Harrison smiled at the question. "That's Sam Greywolf's casino, isn't it?"

"Yes."

"They used to," Harrison nodded, "but of course it's in a blind trust now that he's acquired the football franchise to create the Loggers."

"Do you see any other involvements in our region based on the list of Omni's holdings, Joel?" Abe asked. He expected there were none; therefore, he did not want Joel focused on the information that had emerged to this point. There might be nothing untoward about the tenuous links that seemed to exist between Greywolf's activities and Brockhurst's financial circumstances. Abe did not want to arouse the curiosity of someone who routinely wrote about business matters. Harrison might write something to do either Brockhurst or Greywolf the disservice of creating an unfavorable rumor based on an inference that was reasonable but could not be confirmed.

After a careful scrutiny of the list, Joel shook his head, "I don't see anything else."

"Well, I guess that's the extent of the connections between Brockhurst, Greywolf, and the Omni Corporation. Thanks, Joel."

Abe was certain that his and Joel's employer would be displeased if Abe had stimulated publicity that curtailed Brockhurst's chances at the highest of public offices in the nation.

He had to talk to Adele about how the link between Omni, the Black River Casino, and Brockhurst's former business fit into their theory that the sensational story that Penelope Dayton had approached him about a month ago was about the sources of the funding of the Brockhurst presidential campaign. He thanked Joel for his help and exited quickly before Joel was prompted to ask what had led him to seek information in the first place.

When he reached Adele on her cell phone, she assumed that he was calling to seek a report on her progress. "I'm just getting started, Abe. Obviously, Senator Brockhurst didn't stage Fortner's fatal accident by himself. I'm trying to look into the 'who' of who he might have gotten to arrange it."

"I can give you a very plausible theory about that. I had a piece of luck. Let's meet at the hangout down the street from the Sentinel and I'll fill you in."

As they sat with steaming cups of coffee, Adele listened intently to the Abe's report of an indirect connection between Sam Greywolf and Senator Brockhurst through their separate involvement with Omni Enterprises. She smiled wryly. "So the casino management company that used to operate Greywolf's casino is owned by the same conglomerate that bought Brockhurst's business at a ridiculously high price."

Abe leaned back in his chair and, after a quick look around to confirm that no one was sitting near, said with relish, "That's most likely the information that Harold Fortner whispered into Penelope Dayton's ear in an effort to impress her with his role in big league politics."

Adele nodded thoughtfully. "The connection between Brockhurst and Greywolf through Omni is indirect, Abe. Besides, having made a bad business deal or one that hasn't worked out yet is not illegal."

Abe shook his head in disagreement, "It doesn't matter whether it was Omni that paid Brockhurst three times what his company was worth with their own money or on behalf of Greywolf. It is suspicious. That they were both involved with Omni makes the speculation that Greywolf arranged a pay off to Brockhurst for helping with the franchise acquisition. No one can know whose money came to the senator through the conglomerate.

However, neither Greywolf nor the senator would want the story, even though it's technically legal, to surface."

"So they contained Penelope's effort to sell a story that may or may not be provable by paying her to leave," Adele concluded.

"That probably would have ended the problem, but Fortner came to be viewed as a loose cannon who needed to be eliminated," Abe said. "Or maybe that solution was turned to when an investigative reporter turned out to be better at dodging cars than expected," Abe asserted.

Adele looked skeptical. "That probably never happened, except in the overactive imagination of a less than objective reporter. It's more likely that Fortner got greedy and the people behind Omni are not into any form of 'share the wealth'."

"You know," Abe frowned, "it would not be easy to make the circumstances of Fortner's death look like an accident."

"It would take a specialist, maybe a team of specialists," Adele mused.

"People at a conglomerate with connections to Las Vegas just might have access to such expertise," Abe suggested. "But that part of the scenario is starting to get a little farfetched."

"Maybe," Adele admitted with a sigh. After a brief silence ensued, Adele suggested, "Maybe we should take this to Henry." Abe nodded agreement and reached for the nearby desk phone to see if the editor was available immediately.

After they had told Henry Burton what they knew and what they inferred from it, the editor pursed his mouth in a manner that pulled the corners of his mouth downward in an expression of doubt familiar to all the Sentinel's reporters. The expression said that the editor was unsatisfied with the implications or the substance or the proof of a story that they had brought to him.

"You haven't really got anything but suspicion on which to base a major story of murder, fiscal chicanery, and scandal related to a possible presidential race. The national media wouldn't be able to resist picking up what you speculate if we print a story that might blow up in our faces."

Burton showed disgust in adding, "Unless we have the standards of a supermarket tabloid--and I thank God we don't--we won't be able to produce anything in the way of hard evidence to support the allegations."

"Come on, Henry, our scenario is the only plausible account for what we do know. At the very least, Fortner's death is suspicious," Abe argued.

Adele joined in. "What if we don't print the whole scenario—that is, don't print the strange purchase price of Brockhurst's company, the franchise award to Greywolf and their mutual involvement with the same conglomerate--but dwell only on the mysterious aspects of Fortner's death? We could focus on his unscheduled travel, his not informing his Washington office staff and the consequences for the staff of his consulting business. Maybe some specifics that are part of the wider story will surface. You know how it works, Henry. Turn over a rock and other creepy things start to scurry out from under other rocks nearby."

"Things that crawl out from metaphorical rocks don't sue; real people who are angered by hints in stories that are plausible but unproven always sue. And they most often win, even when they shouldn't," the editor said emphatically.

"Henry," Abe began, drawing out the pronunciation of the name to emphasize his plea, "don't you trust us to write vaguely enough to avoid a successful suit?"

Burton looked from one to the other of his reporters. "I've seen enough of the work of each of you to know that you are both masters of the language of cautious inference and the clever qualifier to know that you won't bluntly assert what you can't prove. The publisher doesn't like successfully defended suits any better than he does unsuccessfully defended ones. The cost of either can be remarkably similar."

"So you're not willing to give him a speech on the role of journalism in an open society?" Abe said in an attempt to combine humor and desperation.

Adele could not avoid rolling her eyes. She focused on Burton intently and asked, "How about telling the boss that it's potentially the biggest story this paper has ever covered, Henry?"

"I'm glad you said 'potentially.' It's also potentially the biggest and most expensive embarrassment that this paper has ever had," the editor pointed out. Besides, are you forgetting that Mr. Etheridge and Senator Brockhurst are personal friends? The paper has endorsed him in every office he's ever run for, including his campaign for the state legislature long before any of the three of us even worked for this paper.

"I don't even have to look it up to believe that he's contributed the legal limit to Brockhurst's campaign in every election. The boss would hold to a higher standard of proof in any story about Brockhurst than he would about anyone else in the universe."

"Won't you at least take the story to him and let him decide, Henry?" Adele pleaded.

Henry looked at the pair earnestly. "Let me explain how an editor retains his credibility with the boss. You keep to a minimum the number of times you take to the publisher a request to do a story that could blow up in the publisher's hands. The boss begins to think that you don't know what 'proof' means."

"Proof?" Abe mused with a tone of disgust. "There's never 'proof' of a conspiracy story like this unless someone confesses." With a complete lack of seriousness, Abe asked, "How about if Adele and I go to Brockhurst or Sam Greywolf and ask them to admit that there was a payoff to get the senator's support for the award of the franchise and the campaign to get the new stadium and that Omni was used as the conduit for the money?"

"And just for a capper," the editor added with feigned gravity, "why don't you ask them to tell us who killed Fortner?"

With equal lack of seriousness equal to the editor's, Adele asked Abe, "What? You're not going to ask if they tried to run down your best buddy and made a high-priced hooker disappear?"

"I'll just ask about the big stuff," Abe said facetiously.

"Tell you what," Henry Burton said amenably. "If you can at least tell me how and where you would go to get proof of your scenario, I'll at least discuss the story with Etheridge."

There was a silence of considerable length. Then Abe offered with a defeated sigh. "How about if we take guns when we go ask for a confession?"

Adele mused, "Maybe there already is something as good as a confession waiting for us." Adele's spontaneous statement took her by as much surprise as it did her listeners. However, as she gave further consideration to her spontaneous utterance, she grinned at the disbelieving pair with a Christmas morning smile.

What she had announced quite spontaneously now began to seem ever more intriguing as she pondered it. She faced Henry Burton to explain her realization. "Fortner's executive assistant said that Fortner put everything in his computer rather than putting it on paper. What if he recorded the same information that he whispered to his playmate, as well as his knowledge of what has happened since, in his computer? If we got our hands on the computer, we might have all the proof we need."

Abe stared out the window, fighting against his own optimism. "If Fortner's death was a murder and not an accident, it was no doubt done by professionals. Surely they would have been instructed to dispose of his computer."

"That would be true only if anyone suspected that there was any compromising information on it," Adele pointed out.

Abe nodded his concession. "If they thought he was safely on the team, maybe they'd assume he'd be smart enough not to record compromising information."

"On the other hand," Burton injected to restrain this new area of speculation, "they knew him as a man who spilled his guts to a hooker."

"Henry," Adele began pleadingly, "we should at least go after the computer to see if they, whoever 'they' are, overlooked the possibility of Fortner having put into the computer what he did not put on paper."

"It's something to take to the boss, Henry, as a lead that justifies our continuing to work on the story," Abe said in support of Adele's argument.

The editor did not pause for long. "I'll have someone do a simple obituary on Fortner. I'll review your scenario for the whole story with the boss--beginning with the call girl's wanting to sell a story--and recommend that you two continue to look into the story by trying to find out if there's anything on Fortner's computer. However, neither of you goes anywhere near this entire story in any way until I get you an O.K. to go after the laptop. Understood?"

Burton glared at them with his best managerial glare. "I mean it. Cross me on this and you'll wish you were never born."

Abe was suitably cowed and did not doubt Adele was as well. Henry was well known for making life unpleasant for journalists who disobeyed his explicit directives. Dismissal was much preferable to further employment under his lash. The pair left the editor's office meekly. Waiting for the elevator, Abe adopted his most sincere demeanor and said, "That was one hell of an idea, thinking of that laptop, Adele."

Adele smiled warmly. "It was your mentioning a confession as our only hope that brought it to mind. Score one for you."

"Score one for us both," Abe said. "We should celebrate. Dinner on me tonight?"

"You're on," Adele responded immediately.

Abe was suddenly flustered at his having made the invitation. He decided to use the stairs rather than wait for the elevator. "Pick you up at seven at your place," he said over his shoulder. He looked back for a moment and caught Adele's broad smile.

Chapter

27

Promptly at seven, Abe appeared at Adele's door. She responded quickly to the bell. Their exchange of greetings was a bit stiff on both sides. When Abe opened the car door for her, he realized that, although he routinely did so for women, this was the first time he did it for Adele even though he had often driven her before.

For their evening's dinner, Abe chose elegance over heartiness, that being a departure from his normal choice for dining out. He had made their reservation at a highly regarded French restaurant that was unexplored territory for him. Adele was obviously pleased. He had not known that Adele had a weakness for French cuisine and was delighted to choose again from a menu with which she was familiar. With her guidance, he was able to choose an entree which he found tolerable. His lack of interest in culinary experimentation became the initial subject of their dinner table banter. However, they seamlessly moved on to a variety of topics from sports to politics to mutual acquaintances that they found either endearing or difficult. Amazingly, their feelings about people, ranging from what made them admirable to what made them absurd, were strikingly similar.

Their conversation lasted much longer than the meal and was continued at a sports bar where they found that their feelings about certain pro basketball players was diametrically opposite. It added zest to the evening that there was an innocuous subject on which to disagree and exchange harmless barbs about. Abe thought it the most pleasant evening he had spent in years and suggested that their unresolved differences over pro basketball players should be explored further over lunch tomorrow.

The next day, it turned out to be a very long lunch, after which they had barely enough time to return to work for a few hours of writing and phone calls that got their journalistic obligations out of the way so that they could enjoy an early dinner together.

It was not surprising, therefore, after their having gravitated to being together so much, that Henry Burton's call found them together over coffee in the staff lounge when he summoned them to his office the morning after their second evening of dining together. Their discussion in the elevator and down the hall to Burton's office centered on how they would approach the problem of getting Harold Fortner's laptop, since they agreed on the inference that Burton had summoned them to tell them they had permission to proceed with their investigation into a possible political scandal.

They both sat in shocked silence, therefore, when the editor told them that they would not be pursuing the Brockhurst-Greywolf story at all. When the extended silence made it obvious that his two reporters were not going to speak, Henry Burton offered a calming gesture of his hand. "Of course, you deserve an explanation. I told the publisher that you suspected that the proof of a story of corruption in both politics and professional sport might be found on Harold Fortner's laptop computer.

He directed me to explore the possibility of access to the information on the computer myself directly with Fortner's senior assistant at Fortner's consulting firm. You know La Plante, the assistant, of course, since he's the one you spoke to about Fortner's death. His initial resistance was weakened by my telling him that we suspected that his boss's death was not an accident. However, it took a substantial fee before he was willing to examine what was stored on the laptop to see if there was anything there that would have made his boss a target. La Plante knew it was Fortner's normal practice to store sensitive information and his personal records and notes under a password known only to himself. Unfortunately, La Plante was unable to work out the password despite hours of trying, so it is impossible to find out if Fortner had recorded anything about illegal or unsavory activity by Brockhurst, Greywolf or the Omni Corporation."

"How about if we took a shot at it?" Abe asked.

Burton nodded slowly. "The new owner of that computer isn't going to let anyone tinker with it now or ever."

"The new owner?" Adele asked.

"Yes," Burton acknowledged with a smile, "the new owner, one Lionel Etheridge, your boss and mine. He wanted it bad enough to make it the most expensive laptop ever sold. The price, in fact, was substantial enough that Fortner's political consulting firm will have the funds to go on without its founder's participation."

"Well, if our publisher owns Fortner's computer, why can't we try to squeeze something out of it?" Adele frowned.

"He has his reasons," Burton said. "Besides, you two each are about to be assigned news stories that I want you to write without the embellishment of speculation." Burton adopted a decisive managerial air and pointed at Adele. "Brockhurst is going to announce that he will not made a run for his party's presidential nomination, and I want you to cover his announcement."

Adele sighed unenthusiastically, "How exciting."

"And you," Burton continued, pointing to Abe, "need to cover Sam Greywolf's announcement later today that he has decided not to involve himself directly in the operation of the Loggers football team and will be seeking a general manager to head the operation."

Abe and Adele looked at one another in astonishment. The stunned reporters turned to the editor. Each struggled to absorb the reality of the stories they were being assigned.

Adele asked with pained surprise, "Brockhurst's not running?"

"And Greywolf's now going to back off to arm's length from the project that has been the sole focus of his life for better than five years?" Abe sputtered. "Are you sure, Henry?"

With a placidity that bordered on boredom, Burton said, "Of course I'm sure." A faint smile lingered on his lips as he looked at his two reporters. He slid a sheet of paper across his desk toward the pair sitting across from him. "These are the times of the press conferences.

Don't be late to them and don't miss the deadline for submitting your stories."

"Henry," Adele and Abe groaned the name in unison.

"What? What?" Burton said with an unconvincing tone for conveying a manager's stern reaction to being challenged by subordinates.

"Come on, Henry," Abe cajoled, "You want us to stand in the middle of all this smoke and not yell 'fire'?"

"Yeh, Henry," Adele injected. "Are we supposed to write these stories and not include any inferences about why each of these guys is doing this?"

Burton displayed a bit of reluctance before he answered. "I will only say that our Lionel Etheridge can be a very persuasive man."

Adele suggested, "I think our publisher's persuasive power was greatly enhanced by the possession of information that would convince a friend, whom he wanted to protect from future embarrassment, that remaining a senator was the wiser course of action."

Abe donned an elaborate expression of thoughtfulness and asked, "You mean if our Lionel may have a laptop with the kind of information that would make his suggestion more like a threat or a command?"

Burton shook a raised finger at the pair. "You two are way ahead of yourselves. I told you that, if there is anything embarrassing to Brockhurst, Greywolf or anyone else on Fortner's laptop, it is inaccessible because it is apparently under a password that defies recognition. And I can tell you with absolute certainty that that is true."

"Of course," Abe stated with a smile, "unless the owner of the laptop in question lets a big time computer geek work on it, everyone will have to take his word for what is or isn't there."

Henry offered an openhanded gesture with arms outstretched to underscore the self-evident fact of what Abe had said.

Concluding that the meeting had reached its substantive end, Adele stood. "Is the boss greatly disappointed that his friend the senator won't be running for president, Henry?"

"Whatever one thinks of Lionel Etheridge's views on the issues, he likes his politics and his politicians to be above board," the editor asserted.

"At least we can be grateful for that," Adele said.

"Yeh," Abe agreed as he stood and stretched, "since he was the only one who could curb the wrongdoing in this case."

"There is the little matter of a possible murder that's not going to be investigated," Adele injected.

"The assertion has been made that a blackmailer had, what was for his victims, a fortunate accident," Henry Burton stated.

"Was Fortner that?" Abe asked with a surprised frown.

"Brockhurst says that he had become an unexpectedly expensive consultant," Burton reported.

Adele shook her head in frustration. "Does it bother anyone else in this room that what passes for justice in this instance is: covering up a series of activities that encompassed political chicanery, financial impropriety and a very suspicious and convenient death has been achieved through vigilante action rather than by the established avenues of justice?"

"Of those here besides you, Adele, it only bothers Henry and me," Abe said with a shrug.

"Unfortunately, in this case, that's the best we can hope for in this wonderful democracy of ours," Burton said with palpable sarcasm.

"So we should *really* start to worry when the power structure has no more Lionel Etheridges in it?" Adele asked sadly.

"Do we think our democracy can count on the Lionel Etheridges in every instance?" Abe mused.

"Let's not even try to answer that one," Burton said, his tone conveying that he intended to conclude the discussion.

As Adele and Abe walked down the hall from Henry Burton's office, Abe said, "Well, I guess we've both got work to do."

"Yes, I guess we'll both be tied up the rest of the day," Adele said.

After they boarded the elevator, they fell into the silent and studious examination of the floor and the ceiling of their conveyance, which is, for some mysterious reason, the universal activity of persons in elevators feeling some tension.

When the elevator reached Adele's floor, Abe held the door open and stayed in place since he was headed for the garage. After Adele had stepped off and begun to walk away, he continued to hold the door open and called after her. When she turned to face him, Abe said, "I know we don't have a story to work on together anymore, but how about dinner this evening?"

Adele nodded and smiled, "Meet you at the Italian place at 7:00?"

Abe returned her nod and smile and let the door close.

Chapter

28

That evening, as they sat sipping the cognac that had been ordered to conclude dinner, they were laughing over their failure to stick to their resolve not to discuss their recently concluded investigation, which each had injected into the conversation several times. "O.K." Abe said with a broad smile that contrasted with the businesslike air he had assumed for the moment, "we've got another subject to dispose of. Let's deal with it and forget about that damned story."

"Actually, I've got something I've got to discuss with you, too," Adele said. "Let me go first." Abe looked resistant until she added a pleading facial expression that Abe had decided several weeks ago was irresistible. It was Adele's only expression with which the bold and confident former jock transformed herself into a cute girl.

Adele lifted her purse from the empty chair where she had placed it at the start of dinner and set it on the table in front of her. "I suppose, with the weighty things that have required your attention of late, that you've forgotten about our little wager. You remember that each of us wrote four columns for the other's byline, and we would see how each of our efforts fared in the market research conducted for the Sentinel that was completed last week?"

"In fact, I haven't forgotten," Abe said. "The deal was that which of us using the other person's byline who got the higher scores from total of the unsolicited comments by readers and the numbers from the focus group interviews would be the winner. The winner is to get a week in the Caribbean at the expense of the other writer."

"Right," Adele agreed. "I got so wrapped up in the Brockhurst story that I never checked until today on the final set of scores to know who'd won. Up to that point our scores were close enough that the outcome could have gone either way depending on the last set of scores."

Abe smiled with satisfaction. "That's my recollection going into the last exchange of bylines too."

Adele delved into her bag. "Well, in view of the way our contest turned out, this is for you." She set a small folder on the table in front of Abe. "Congratulations. I hope that you enjoy your week in the sun." She bowed her head in a brief nod of deference and said, "You do good work, Abe."

Abe stared at her and frowned, "What are trying to pull, Friedman?"

Adele pushed the travel folder closer to Abe's side of the table and said, "There are your paid up travel arrangements for a week in the Caribbean on me."

"No, no, no," Abe responded with a schoolmasterish shake of his finger. "I'm certain that the scores just didn't turn out that way. The truth is," Abe continued as he reached into his sport jacket inside pocket and placed on the table a folder identical to the other. "The fourth effort figures no doubt put you clearly out front. You're a damn fine writer, and I'm not ashamed to admit it." He put his folder beside Adele's plate. "There are your paid travel arrangements for a week in the Caribbean."

"Hey," Adele objected with a chuckle, "I don't accept charity, Fuller. You won fair and square."

"Don't give me that," protested Abe with an air of good humor. "You obviously misinterpreted the data." He picked up the folder that Adele had set before him and handed it toward her.

"No way I'm taking that back," Adele said. "I went to a lot of work to make those arrangements. Everything is set: plane reservations and the rest of the package, including your choice among three islands on which the hotel chain has a resort."

Abe dropped the travel folder Adele had given him on top of the one he had set beside Adele's place for her. "You have plenty of time to cancel everything and get your money back."

"The same goes for you," Adele responded and picked up the folders and reached them toward Abe.

Abe refused to accept them and said, "O.K., this obviously isn't getting us anywhere. Let's get to a computer and check out the scores and we'll see who knows how to combine numerical scores and accompanying comments to a sensible conclusion."

Adele smiled confidently and said, "Apparently I am not yet finished teaching you some of the finer arts of journalism. My place is closer. Shall we go?"

Abe rose from his chair and said, "I can hardly wait. I'll track down our waiter and pay the check so that we can be on our way."

Chapter

29

As quickly as permitted by their unnecessary expenditure of time asserting to one another who would prove to be correct, Adele and Abe were eventually seated before her computer. Adele was about to access the survey results when Abe stopped her. "Wait a minute. I want to re-read your last column under my byline again before we look at the scores." Sliding over into the chair that Adele vacated, Abe accessed the previous week's edition that carried the last column that Adele had written under his name.

After a quick reading, Abe shook his head and chided Adele, "You got to be kidding me, Friedman. This is doubtlessly a thoughtful and well-written piece, but it's not a column that is going to produce favorable reader comments or even high numerical evaluations either. What a downer for the fans of a soon-to-be-launched new pro football franchise to read."

"Really?" Adele asked. "You don't think the Tampa Bay analogy has any relevance?"

"I don't contest that it is possible that the Loggers, in their early years, may be as painful to watch as the Tampa Bay Buccaneers were in their early years."

"Define 'early,'" Adele said. "The Buccaneers stacked up so many losing seasons that some people concluded they would never have a season where they won more than they lost, let alone ever make the playoffs."

"Yeh, it took a while, I admit," Abe agreed, "but you didn't even mention that they finally won a super bowl. God, Adele, to dwell on this subject for an entire column, one would think you were trying to throw our little contest."

"Oh, don't be ridiculous," Adele said as she shooed Abe out of her chair. "I'm going to take another look at the last column you wrote for me." She accessed the column and gave it a quick reading as Abe had done to her work. "Oh, my God," she sputtered, "Talk about downer columns. I'll be lucky if I don't get stoned by the voters who read this column. You couldn't have done better if you had been trying to produce low scores. This charming lecture asserts that the electorate has damn near completed the destruction of democracy in this country by their failure to turn out to vote, even in presidential elections, let alone off-year elections. You may have made it impossible for me to go out of doors for several months."

"Yeh, well my assertions are painfully true, and they were overdue for it being said," Abe responded firmly.

Adele smiled and pointed an accusing finger at Abe, "You tried to throw the bet, Fuller."

"I did not. Though I'll admit it is the kind of piece that it takes a while for people to warm up to," Abe said with an exaggerated air of superiority.

"Yeh, well your little game of throw-the-match isn't going to work," Adele stated sternly, "If I had read this before, I'd have declared the bet off a week ago."

Abe's eyebrows arched in surprise. "Wait a minute. Did you just say you hadn't read the column before now?"

Adele waved off the question. "A slip of the tongue."

"Really? Then how were you so certain that the scores would be in my favor that you bought me a ticket to the Caribbean?" Abe challenged.

Adele showed no contrition. "I was sure the same way you were so certain I'd won that you bought trip tickets for me. Admit it,

Abe Fuller," Adele accused. "You were sure I'd won because you intentionally tanked your column."

"Ridiculous," Abe snorted. "I am just trying to be a gracious loser. Stop trying to complicate things and get ready to take your vacation. I went to a lot of trouble to get that particular plane reservation."

"That particular plane reservation?" Adele repeated with curiosity. She took out of her purse the travel packet that Abe had offered her in the restaurant.

After a brief scrutiny, she said, "The plane reservation is for the day after Christmas with a return flight the day after New Year."

"Right," Abe said. "It was the only week that Henry Burton told me that you could have off."

"You asked Henry to schedule a week's vacation for me?" Adele said with puzzlement in her voice.

"Of course," Abe responded. "How else could I get the travel agent to set the package up to match your work schedule? Henry insisted that that was the only week you could have off."

"Look at the flight reservations I made of you," Adele said with a wry smile and handed Abe the travel folder she had given him earlier.

After a quick look, Abe frowned and said, "The same week."

"Yeh," Adele said. "Henry said that that was the only week you could have off."

There was an extended period of silent eye contact between the two. Finally Abe said haltingly, "Apparently Henry thinks that you and I are…"

"Apparently," Adele said.

There was another extended silence during which both parties looked a bit nervous. "We could each pick a different island," Abe suggested meekly.

"You want to do that?" Adele asked with a look that seemed to Abe able to see into his heart.

"No."

Adele held out her hand to take back the travel packet that she had given him. "What me to pick out an island for both of us?"

Abe handed over the packet without comment. He was sure his smile gave the answer.

Adele put both travel packets in her purse and said, "Why don't you get us a couple brandies from the cabinet over there while we discuss whether I'm supposed to ask for one room or two."

Abe started toward the cabinet and turned around to ask, "Am I going to survive this vacation?"

"I think that you might have an even chance," Adele responded, her eyes showing a mixture of humor and intrigue that delighted Abe.

"My chances are that good?" Abe asked with a grin that showed his delight. "This could be the best deal I've ever been offered."

"This is definitely the best deal you'll ever get in your lifetime," Adele said with a toss of her hair.

Abe's grin looked to become permanent, his mind already focused on possible delights. "I'm convinced of it."

Adele face fixed into a serious expression.. "Be clear that it's a once in a lifetime offer."

"I think it's the one I've been waiting for all my life," Abe said. He started to go for the brandy but stopped in a few steps and turned toward Adele. "I have one condition." Abe pointed toward Adele for emphasis. "We will never play a game of one-on-one basketball."

"But we always have a tournament at the family reunion every summer," Adele complained.

"That's when your father will be showing me his previous season's game films," Abe said.

"Oh, right," Adele said. "How could I have forgotten?"